I0562878

The Searching Place

A Novel by

F.J. Thomas

Solstice Publishing - www.solsticepublishing.com

To all the gals who have gone through tough times but come out swinging like a cowgirl.

Chapter One

Lily glanced at her phone for the hundredth time and sighed as she opened a bottle of cheap red wine. Her managing agent should have called over an hour ago. Her whole entire life was riding on this deal with Millington Press. It had to happen.

She jumped as her phone vibrated on the end of the counter. She took a deep breath and calmed her nerves as she picked it up.

"Lil, are you sitting down?"

"I am now." Lily sat her glass of wine on the coffee table, then sank down into the leather sofa. It was the last piece of decent furniture she owned.

"For goodness sake Nate, just spit it out. You know I can't handle suspense, especially after all the hell I've been through the last week." She took another sip of courage.

Nate released the sigh he was holding and finally said the words that made him sick to his stomach. "Millington Press scrapped your book."

His words sucked the air right out of the room, taking all her hope with it.

"What? What do you mean they, well you, scrapped my book? I thought this was a done deal… You know I had everything counting on this book. I can't…" Try as she might, she just couldn't hold back the tide of tears even with the help of the wine.

"I know. I know you needed this. Shhhh…. Don't cry…. Please don't cry, Lil," he begged.

"I just thought…" she blubbered out between sobs.

"You know you're one of my favorite writers– well, more than that. You're a friend. I try my best to look out for you. I always have. Trust me, I tried hard, but they had to cut some books and well... how do I say this?" He swallowed. "It just wasn't your best work."

"Well what can you expect after all the pressure I've been under?" she bawled and took another sip of wine as she swiped the tears creeping down one cheek.

"I know, but you've got to be a writer first and foremost if you're going to do this for a living. You can't go off the deep end every time your personal life goes all to pieces. You know that."

"Yes, I know that. I thought considering what I'm going through right now that story was pretty good."

"The story was good. It was the writing that sucked. Sorry." He winced. Maybe he shouldn't have said it quite that way.

"Leave it to you to make me feel better when my life is going to hell in a handbasket!" she wailed.

"Well, it's true. You know I'm nothing but truthful with you." He had been, for the most part.

"Yeah, you're not one to blow smoke up my skirt!"

"You wanted honesty and that's what you got. Besides, I think Jan would take offense to that."

Lily sighed. "I know. I just don't know what I'm going to do."

"Lil, this makes what? The fifth divorce you've gone through?"

"Thanks for reminding me." She needed another drink.

"Well, what I'm saying is that this isn't anything new for you. Why are you letting it impact your writing and your life?"

"I write romances, remember?"

"Yeah, but you're better than that. I know you are. Snap out of it and fight. Don't lose your career over another man in your life." Of course, one might argue that man was what had been her muse in the first place.

She sighed hopelessly. "I just don't know what I'm going to do this time. I don't have anything or anyone to fall back on. James completely wiped me out. Heck, I even lost most of the furniture. My book sales are slowing down, and I haven't won a barrel race in I don't know how long." God, her life really was going to hell.

"Look, what you need is something to get your creative juices going again."

"That normally requires the male species or a good barrel race but I think I'd better swear those two things off for a while," she told him.

"What you need is a change of scenery. You need to get out and get away from all this and find your muse."

"Short of a good pair of a wranglers, what do you suggest?"

"Well, is there somewhere you've always wanted to write about?" he asked.

Lily thought for a moment. All the settings in her books had been in the West, which she was very familiar with, but she'd always been curious about the East.

"What about the Appalachian Mountains?"

"I hear banjo music," Nate laughed. "Hey, if that's what brings out your curiosity, go for it."

"Well, I hear they have a lot of barrel racing in Tennessee. I'd have a chance maybe to win some money. Might be just what I need," she reasoned.

"Okay, what town?"

"I don't know. The only towns I've heard of are Nashville and Knoxville. Knoxville is closer to the mountains."

"Well, then Knoxville it is," he told her.

"This is kind of exciting." She giggled, feeling a little better for the moment.

"Yep, a new adventure is just what you need."

"Thanks, Nate."

"For what? Telling you your book was cancelled because your writing sucked?" he asked.

Lily laughed. "No, for yanking a knot in my tail and telling me to snap out of it."

"Hey, that's what friends and agents are for. Well, I have to go. Jan's ready and we're going out to eat. Let me know where you're at once you get settled. We can talk about your new book idea if you want."

"Ok. Have fun and tell Jan I said hi."

"I will. Be careful."

Lily set the phone on the coffee table, then reached up and smoothed the mass of fiery red curls back from her face. She grabbed her laptop, one of the few things she still had that was worth anything, and turned it on.

Deep down she knew Nate was right, on all accounts. Her last book had sucked. She'd let James take everything, including her writing ability. How many times was she going to do this?

She'd been through it five times already, chasing her heart and some ideology of the romance that she wrote about. Each time it took away another piece of her heart and a piece of that romantic idea that she so badly wanted to believe in but was coming to harshly realize didn't exist.

A new start in a new town might be just what she needed to get her fire back and believe in life again. A girl could only take so much dust and brown before it started to wear on her. Mountains of green sounded like the perfect fix.

She pulled up Google on her computer and took another sip of wine to keep the courage flowing. Moving clear across the country on her own sounded like a wonderful adventure, but the reality was her money was running low and it wasn't just her she had to think about.

Mercado, her palomino gelding, needed a place to stay as well and board was expensive in most parts of the country. She'd have to find a place for him that she could afford, at least until she wrote the next bestseller.

After an hour of surfing on the net, all the places she'd found to rent were still out of her price range, even though she'd learned the cost of living in east Tennessee was lower than what she was used to.

She had to find something fast as she had to be out of the condo by the end of the week. She made a last-ditch effort and pulled up Craigslist. Suddenly an ad caught her eye.

House for rent with small barn and paddock. $650.00 per month, Willowcreek area. Reduced rate if you occasionally help with farm chores. Email sfischer@hotmail.com for details.

"Hmmm. It's definitely affordable and in my price range. I wonder where Willowcreek is…"

Lily pulled up a Google search and quickly learned that Willowcreek was south of Knoxville and not far off the interstate.

"Cheap and convenient. That just might work." She said as she tucked her leg underneath her and sent the email.

Almost immediately, her computer notified her that she had a message in her inbox. Her stomach jumped in anticipation.

As she opened the picture attachments, Lily understood why the rent was so cheap. Her heart sank.

Although it was certainly habitable, the house was a small simple concrete block dwelling very similar to the migrant houses she'd seen. The barn was a low run-in shed that looked like it hadn't been used in ages, and the fencing was rusted barbed wire that looked as though it would fall down at any moment. The only good thing was that there was plenty of bright green grass that would save her money on hay.

Her dream castle in a new land was rather disappointing. Not long ago she had lived on one of the finest ranches in Phoenix with one of the most well-known Cutting Horse breeders in the country. Now, here she was seriously considering living in a migrant house with a shed and barbed wire. How did she ever let herself get to this point?

The truth was she was flat broke and didn't have a choice. She had to do something, and her options were few. She didn't want to go work in fast food, which at this point was looking better all the time, but she wasn't a good enough jockey to find a decent job riding in Texas either. Writing fiction was the only marketable talent she had left, and that was questionable at the moment.

She couldn't stay out in this dusty hell hole and hope that she could turn out a new book that was good enough. She had to get to somewhere affordable that inspired her best work and she didn't have long to do it. Her finances were dwindling fast which meant she had to put herself on a budget and a deadline.

"Nothing like being the starving artist to bring out a little inspiration and your best work." She clicked Reply and told the owner she'd take it.

***

Making such a long journey alone was intimidating but sometimes a girl had to just cowgirl up and get it done. Well, at least that's what she was telling herself, and it helped most of the time. Two flat tires and another two days later, Lily and Mercado rolled off of Interstate 75 on to the Willowcreek exit. She had put new the address just off Cotton Town road into her GPS but the property owner, Susan, warned her that although she didn't use such things, it was her understanding that those GPS contraptions don't pick up places "out in the sticks".

Not to be deterred, Lily put the address into her phone. It had brought her this far; surely getting to Cotton Town and then Fischer road shouldn't be too hard. Susan had said the house was about ten miles off the interstate, but the GPS had only shown seven. Lily decided that the GPS was probably right and tucked Susan's directions into the sun visor while she listened to "Rachael", as she called the voice on her phone, give her the instructions for her next move.

She quickly found Cotton Town road and turned by an old block store that looked as though it had seen better days with its stained block walls, half-fallen porch roof, and rusted railing.

Her phone had indicated that Fischer road should be five miles on the left. When it came time to turn left however, there was no Fischer road. A little further down, the road forked and became narrow. Frustrated, Lily pulled her truck and trailer into the first driveway and pulled out the directions from the sun visor. She studied her hand scribbled notes. There were no more clues than the GPS.

She was lost in her thoughts when suddenly she jumped at the tap on her window. She pushed the button on the door and caught her breath as the window rolled down.

"Can you move your truck? You're in the way." A tall lanky man pointed at the road.

Lily stole a quick look at the tanned stranger and then turned to see what he was pointing at. It was a load of round bales on a flatbed trailer.

"Look, if you can't back that thing around, I can move it for you," he told her.

Yes, he was good looking and even in a pair of Wranglers, which she didn't expect, but how dare he assume that just because she was a female that she couldn't back her trailer around! Wait. She did have enough room, right?

She checked her mirrors and then asked, "You know where Fischer Road is?"

He laughed, revealing a disarming smile. "You used your GPS, didn't ya." It was more of a statement than a question.

"Yes, how did you know…Ohhh... Susan was right, I guess?"

He nodded. "They don't pick up too well out here. Fischer Road is three miles back on the right, not the left. It leads back to the Fischer dairy farm."

"Dairy farm?"

"Why, yeah. You're looking for Fischer Road. That's the only place that road leads to."

Good Lord, what would her old Phoenix high society friends think about her now living on a dairy farm? In a worker's house, of all places!

"Look, I need to get this load of hay off the road before some young punk comes around that curve and plows into the back of it. You gonna move this thing or you need me to?"

How quickly his mood could turn! One minute he was laughing at her for using a GPS and the next he was riding her for not moving the trailer quick enough.

"I'm going!" She scowled and raised her window up but not before she stole another quick look at the rude farmer walking back to his truck. "Not bad. Not bad…at all."

Much to her relief, she was able to back her horse trailer into the road and get it turned around. After such a long trip, she wasn't sure she could have stood the humiliation of asking for help to operate her own vehicle.

As she pulled by the load of hay, she attempted to wave at the handsome farmer, but he was already focused on pulling forward into the driveway. She felt rather stupid as she lowered her hand, and then thought it best to reset her trip odometer. Maybe this time she'd find Fischer Road. Next time she would have to take better directions!

Just as the man had promised, it was three miles down on the other side of the road. Fortunately, the entrance was wide enough for her truck and trailer to make the turn, but driving was slow as the road was pitted with potholes from wear.

About a mile in, she saw the little block house from the email. It was even less inviting in person with its plain worn gray walls and faded green tin roof. The only plus was that there was plenty of room to pull her rig in and turn it around. That was mainly due to the lack of landscaping.

She pulled the truck into the driveway, cut the engine and then released her seat belt. She breathed a deep sigh.

Suddenly she heard her phone vibrate. It was a message from Nate.

Where are you? Did you make it?

She smiled. At least one person in the world cared about her. She responded that she'd just pulled in the driveway.

She'd been driving non-stop since Memphis and was worn out. She sat for just a moment taking it all in. "So, this is going to be home for a while."

It wasn't what she was used to, but then again, that was the whole point, wasn't it? She just hoped all this wasn't another wild-haired mistake. She had to make this work, no matter how bad it got.

She knew Mercado was just as tired as she was, so her first priority was to get him settled in. Expecting to have to make a few repairs and knowing Mercado would need to acclimate slowly to the grass, she'd had the forethought to bring several livestock panels with her.

A few moments later, she unloaded Mercado and tied him to the trailer until she could get his pen set up. She walked out to the pasture and shed to figure out where she wanted to place the panels for now. The fescue and orchard grass were already knee high and so thick that it was difficult to walk through. If nothing else, the place had enough grass that she may not even have to feed Mercado anything else.

As she neared the front of the shed, she was pleased to find that although low, it was still structurally sound. She was also thrilled to see the ground covered in thick pine shavings. Bedding was the one thing she'd forgotten to grab in her haste to get out of town.

She glanced around to see if there was any water nearby. She didn't see any hydrants sticking up out of the ground but did see an old rusted faucet on the back of the house by the small porch. She would have to run a hose to get water to the shed, but it wasn't too far.

She'd brought six panels with her. With a little effort and some rope, she managed to fit them together in front of the shed to make a large area for Mercado to move around until she had a chance to fully check and fix the fence.

She led the palomino horse back to the makeshift pen and took off his halter. The first thing he did, as she expected, was roll in the soft deep shavings. She rested her chin on the panel rail as she watched her gelding wiggle back and forth and then heave himself upright. She let out a big sigh as she watched him walk over to check out the water bucket and take a long drink. There was something peaceful about watching him settle in.

The gelding then checked out the edge of the enclosure, took a large bite of the bright green grass and kept walking. Suddenly Lily heard the familiar high-pitched clinking sound.

"Dang it. I thought your shoes would last at least another couple of weeks until I could save a little more money and find a decent farrier." Why was it that everything seemed to be falling apart, including her plans for her horse's feet?

A little while later Lily was busy unloading boxes when a rusted red truck pulled into the driveway. She watched as an older but stout, gray haired woman stepped out and held out her hand.

"You must be Lily," the woman said.

Lily noticed her firm grip. "Indeed I am. And you must be Susan?"

"Yep, that's me." Susan looked at the open door of the trailer, walked over and picked up a box.

"You don't have to help me, you know," Lily sheepishly told her.

"Oh, I know, but I know what it's like to be on your own." She laughed, "Besides, I'm nosy."

"I'll be honest, there's not a whole lot to see."

"Honey, I figured as much with you movin' into this ol' place."

Lily gave her a curious look.

"Most of my renters have been women going through a hard time and they needed a place for their horse. They can't afford the high rent in Knoxville, so they come here." She smiled. "I call it 'The Searchin' Place'."

"The Searching Place, huh?"

"Yep, everybody's searchin' for something when they come here, whether they know it or not." She followed Lily into the kitchen. "You'll find what you're searchin' for too, even if you don't know what it is."

Lily tried to stem the crimson creeping into her cheeks. How in the world did this woman that she'd just met size her up so well? Maybe it was the same way she knew about the GPS.

"Oh, I didn't mean to embarrass ya!" She set the box she was holding down and grabbed Lily's hands. "I just want you to feel at home here for however long that's gonna be. That's all. You need anything at all, you just holler at me." She turned and pointed at the side window. "I'm right up that hill there at the top of the ridge, not far at all."

Lily felt her cheeks go three shades hotter. "I...uh... don't know what to say. Thank you."

"You don't have to thank me. That's what we do around here." She absently smoothed the front of her tee shirt. "Well, I guess I'd better get out of here and let you get settled. Holler if you need anything."

Lily nodded silently and watched as Susan walked towards the old diesel truck. She was lost in thoughts of how nice the other woman had been when she suddenly remembered Mercado's shoes.

"Susan, wait!" Lily dashed out into the driveway to catch Susan before it was too late.

The older lady had already turned the truck around and was just about ready to pull out on to the narrow road when she looked up and saw Lily wildly waving her arms. The old farm truck jerked to a halt as Susan slammed on the brakes.

Lily ran all the way to the door. "I almost forgot! I need a farrier for my horse!"

"I know just the fella. Carter Shelton. He lives right down the road. I'll give him a call and tell him you're needing your horse done."

"But..." She appreciated the sentiment and didn't want to appear ungrateful, but she was very picky about who worked on Mercado's feet. He wasn't an old nag that could stand up to the rigors of poor shoeing. No, Mercado was a bit of a hothouse flower in that he had to be shod at just the right angle or he was lame.

"Oh, don't you worry about it! I'll have him come up tomorrow afternoon. He should have finished getting up hay today, and I'm sure he'll work you in. He owes me a favor or two anyhow." With that, she let off the clutch and steered the truck towards home.

Chapter Two

It was nine in the morning when the sound of a truck door slamming in her driveway startled Lily out of her restful sleep. She shut her eyes against the morning sun coming in through the blinds and felt around for her cell phone to find out the time, which was much too early in her book.

"Who could be here this early...I'm not even dressed!" She hurled the covers back and jumped out of bed, scrambling to find anything she could use to cover herself. She knew she should have taken the time to dig through boxes to find her pajamas last night!

Not able to quickly find anything to wear, she pulled the comforter off the bed and wrapped it around her as she scrambled to the living room and peeked through the shades. Parked in her front yard was a red and white truck with a small rusted white horse trailer behind it.

"What the...Somebody better not be stealing my horse!" Of course, what could she do? She was half naked and didn't own a gun. Maybe she could flash them to death?

She ran to the kitchen and jerked open the door. In her haste to get down the narrow little concrete steps, the comforter wrapped around her legs sending her tumbling head over heels into the thick grass below.

Carter Shelton cocked his head to the side and admired the shapely buttocks that were peeking out from the edge of the jumbled mess of dark fluffy material.

"Ya know, I don't think I've ever quite been mooned in such a fashion as this." The bright white set of teeth stood out against his tanned skin as a he grinned.

"You better not be stealing my horse, you..." she hissed. In her effort to stand up and keep herself covered, she only managed to lose her grip on her last piece of decency and fell again, this time exposing her top.

"Oh, to heck with it! It's not like you've never seen a woman's naked body before, I'm sure!" She dropped the tangled mass of material to the ground and stepped out of it, exposing herself. So maybe flashing would be the only weapon she had. Someday she'd have to get a gun, especially after this fiasco!

Carter laughed heartily as he crossed his arms and leaned back against the trailer. His cocky smirk just made her even more furious.

"I mean it! You're not taking my horse! He's the last thing that I have, and I'll fight you for him if I have to!" Lily yelled.

"And... I'm sorry, what are you going to fight me with? You know, I don't think I've ever been greeted with curves quite like this." He was enjoying this just a little too much.

Now free of the danger of tripping again, Lily grabbed the comforter and wiggled it around her. "I'm not sure, but I can be mean if I have to!"

"I guess I'd better set the record straight before you give me a whoopin' I might enjoy a little too much."

Lily opened her mouth, but no words could come out.

"Look lady," he laughed, "I'm just here to shoe your horse. That's it. But now, if you're keen on fighting me, that can be arranged, although I'm not sure I'd fight for this nag." He figured he'd had enough fun for the moment. "I'm assuming that's your yeller' horse back in the shed?"

"Uh...yeah." Deflated, she felt utterly ridiculous and held tighter to the comforter that she wished she could somehow disappear into.

"Does your horse tie?"

"What?"

"Does he tie?"

"Yes, he ties!" Did he think she was an idiot? "Wait... I know you! You're that guy that thought I couldn't back my own trailer yesterday!"

"Yes, I am. And I might say you do a fine job of backing but walking you seem to have a little trouble with."

"Yes, he ties."

"Well, I'll tie him to that peach tree out in the front yard by my truck if that's alright with you. I need a little shade."

Suddenly she remembered the fact that Mercado couldn't be shod by just anyone. "Wait. What credentials do you have?"

"What do you mean credentials? I've been shoeing all my life."

"But what shoeing school did you graduate from?"

"School of hard knocks, that's what school I graduated from. Look, lady." He tipped his hat back on his head just a tad. "If you want some big degree for shoeing you can get someone else to shoe your horse."

"I'm not saying you're not qualified, it's just that my horse has to be shod just right or he's lame."

"Do you want me to shoe him or not?" He pointed down the road as he spoke. "I can go on down the road to the next client. I'm sure they won't moon me when I pull in the driveway."

He had a point, and her horse was overdue if she was going to run anywhere soon. "No, go ahead and shoe him." She hoped she didn't regret it – in times past she had.

"Look, I've been shoeing ever since I was old enough to pick up a horse's foot. I think I can figure out how your horse needs to be shod." He grabbed the halter on the edge of the gate and gave Lily another look. "Tell ya what, if you'll get some clothes on, if you don't like my shoeing, I'll owe you lunch. How's that?"

"Free lunch, huh?"

"Yeah, but that's only if you get our clothes on. I don't think people would take too kindly to a naked woman while they're eatin'"

Lily scowled at him. "Alright." She turned, headed towards the house and tripped once again.

"Careful. Walkin' can be tricky for some people."

She turned to give him a hateful look but was met with a wink that for some reason quickly cooled her jets. Fortunately, she managed to make it the rest of the way to the house and up the steps without embarrassing herself further.

Once inside, she quickly slammed the door behind her and went in search of some clothes to wear, which unfortunately were still packed up in boxes. After several futile attempts to crack open the top of some taped boxes, she decided she'd just wear the same clothes she'd worn the day before.

A few moments later she went to the small bathroom to freshen up. At least her toothbrush wasn't packed in a cardboard box sealed with enough duct tape to survive a fall from an airplane.

Teeth brushed, she focused on getting her curly mane under control with a scrunchy. She studied her reflection in the mirror and fought the urge to slap on some makeup. The long trip from the last couple of days had taken its toll in the form of dark puffy circles under her eyes. Thirty-five was hell, or maybe it was that glass of wine she'd had to put her to sleep? Either way, why couldn't she be twenty again?

"Speaking of age," she said to herself in the mirror, "wonder how old he is…"

Carter looked old enough that she didn't think she'd be considered a cougar but at the same time she wasn't so sure. At any rate, she had to admit he was one fine specimen for any age, even if he did embarrass her first thing this morning.

Wait. What was she thinking? She had no idea if Carter was taken or not. From what she had heard they married young in this part of the country and good men were hard to find. Of course, it depended on what your definition of "good" was. She also didn't need the entanglement of any male right now. She needed to quit this line of thinking.

She grabbed her clothes piled on the floor at the foot of the bed and wiggled into them, almost falling twice. Maybe he was right – she was kind of a klutz.

A few moments later she was appropriately dressed and out the door. As she stepped off the porch, she noticed Carter had already tied Mercado to the tree and was in the process of pulling his front shoes. She also couldn't help but notice the wrangler patch in just the right spot as he bent over and put Mercado's front leg between his knees.

"Who'd you get to shoe this horse last time?" Carter asked over his shoulder as he tugged at the edge of the loosened shoe with the pullers.

"Sam Eldridge back in Texas. Why?"

"Well, I hope you didn't pay much because his shoeing job sucks."

How dare he insult her favorite farrier first thing! She put her hands on her hips. "He's one of the best out there. What makes you think you can do a better job?" She thought it best not to the mention the fact that Sam had been a little too eager to shoe her horse in the first place.

"Well, for one I know how to size a horse. This horse's shoes are a size too small. No wonder you had trouble." He slid Mercado's leg to the ground and stood up. "Two, this horse doesn't have the same angle on any of his feet. He's all over the place."

He tugged on Mercado's lead to pull him up even. "Take a close look at those angles and look at the difference between the feet."

She squatted down and looked at the striped hooves. He was right. All four feet were on completely different angles. Why hadn't she noticed that before? Oh wait...maybe it was because she was too busy flirting back with Sam to notice. "You're right. Absolutely right, Carter."

He gave her a big grin as he tipped his hat back. "I think you'll be satisfied with everything I do."

Fighting the blood flowing up to her cheeks, and to other places, she put her hands on her hips and met his gaze head on. "Don't be so sure about satisfying me. You're not done yet."

He grinned as he picked up another foot. "I was talking about the horse."

She felt her face grow hot and decided it was time to gain some distance by leaning on the trailer wheel well.

"So, I take it after our uh, meeting a little while ago, that Susan didn't tell you I was coming to shoe your horse?" he asked her as he gave a tug on the half-loosened shoe.

"She told me your name and said you would shoe him for me, but it would be in the afternoon. Didn't tell me anything else."

"Nothing to tell, really. I just shoe horses. She didn't tell me your name, just that you were renting and had a horse that needed shoes. I was free this morning, so I figured I'd come over and get him done before it got too hot."

"Everyone has a story, Carter." The writer in her noted the sudden stiffness in his shoulders at her remark. "Anyhow, my name is Lily Perkins. I write books under the name Lillie Starr." She wasn't exactly sure why she had to tell him all of that. It must have been loneliness, but most likely it was just the effect he was having on her.

"Ohhh... so you're one of those writer types."

Why in the world did he have a way of making her feel like a complete idiot? "I guess you could say that."

Lily expected to him have some kind of witty comeback, but instead he just focused on rasping down the hoof he'd just placed on the shoeing stand. She wasn't sure what was more unnerving – suffering under his close scrutiny and quick wit or complete silence. At least when he was silent with his back turned to her, she could enjoy the view... and what a view it was!

She noticed that there wasn't a band on his hand. But then again how likely was it that a healthy working cowboy his age would be single in this part of the country? Real cowboys were few and far between here, or so she'd heard. The writer side of her immediately perked up. If he was single, there just had to be a reason. He must have some personality flaw or maybe a shady past. Of course, with her track record she'd probably find out why first hand. She just couldn't resist a cowboy with issues in Wranglers, no matter how hard she tried. That's what had brought here her to this God forsaken county in the first place!

Suddenly Mercado pulled back as Carter was hammering a nail into his shoe. Lily was jerked out of her thoughts as well and suddenly wondered if she'd been thinking out loud.

"Dammit." Carter winced as Mercado ripped his hoof out from between his knees. Biting the nails in his mouth and gathering his composure as best he could, he reached for Mercado's foot a second time and held it a moment before he started hammering.

Lily released her breath and then asked, "What do you think make him pull?"

"He's probably sore from those small shoes he had on!" he snapped.

"Well, he normally doesn't pull back. He usually stands still."

Carter sighed and stopped nailing. "Look, do you want me to shoe this horse or do you want to do it? It's gettin' hot and I'll be glad to let you take over."

"I was only asking you what you thought. You don't have to be so hateful...or so insecure about your shoeing."

Before Carter could come back with a reply, she stood up and stomped towards the house. True cowboy or not, she wasn't going to tolerate his smart ass remarks.

She slammed the door behind her as she stepped into the kitchen. Her heart racing from being so angry, she resolved that she needed something to do to kill the time so she wouldn't go back outside. The whole house needed unpacking and the kitchen was just as good as any place to start.

Her coffee pot and coffee were the first things she came to. She decided a good hot cup of coffee might be just the thing she needed to turn her mood around. A few moments later the strong aroma of brewing filled the small room and Lily was lost in determining where everything went.

She was unpacking when she heard a knock on the door. She took her time to answer and then opened the door to a hot, sweaty Carter. She felt a slight twinge of pity.

"Come on in. It's at least a little cooler in here." She turned her back to him and pretended to be busy filling the drawers with kitchen stuff.

"Your horse is done. I put him back in the stall. Look, I'm sorry I snapped at you."

She wheeled around. "I guess you do that to all your clients and they just take it from you?"

"Ouch. That hurt." He couldn't meet her fiery gaze. "Ok, you've got me. I'm sorry. I shouldn't have talked to you the way I did. He raked me pretty good when he pulled back and I was pissed off."

"Gotta hand it to you, that's some apology," she said, turning her back on him once again.

"Anybody ever call you the ice princess?"

She shut the drawer a little harder than she intended and faced him. "Yes, I've been called that a time or two when I'm really mad."

"Well, I'm trying to apologize to you... over something basically stupid."

"Stupid? You call talking to me like that something stupid that I shouldn't get upset over?"

"Good grief, you sound like my girlfriend and we just met!"

"Oh? So you have a girlfriend?" Now maybe she'd find out what she'd been wondering about, although his attitude made her wonder why she even cared.

"Well...no, I don't. But..."

"Why not? Maybe it has something to do with that sharp tongue of yours? Or maybe, just maybe it has to do with the fact that you don't respect women and don't know how to talk to them?" She set her shoulders back and casually leaned against the counter.

He shook his head, "I don't have a girlfriend because I don't want one!"

"What? You don't like women? Oh, that's it!" she mocked.

He shifted his feet. "No, that's not it! I like women. Lots of women!"

"So you're a man whore?"

"No, I'm not that either!" he shouted.

A twisted part of her enjoyed seeing him uncomfortable and being on the control side of this little game for a change. "Well, if you're not gay, and you're not a man whore bedding everything you can get your hands on, then why don't you have a girlfriend? What kind of crazy issues do you have, Carter?"

He pointed at her. "I'm not talking about this!"

"What? You're afraid to? Do you have issues?" She grinned from ear to ear as she watched him throw up his hands and shake his head. He wasn't going to answer.

"Ok I'll let you off the hook, this time. But the writer in me will question you harder next time."

"We'll see about that," he replied.

"Yes, we will. Now, do you want a cup of coffee or do you want to just take your money and go? Sounds like I'm paying a prostitute." She giggled as she saw the red rise up his cheeks.

"I guess I'll take the money for my services and go." He gave her a smartass grin. "I'm running a little late. It's seventy-five."

"That's not bad. I'm used to paying a hundred and that's with a deal," she told him.

"I'm not going to ask what kind of deal you got."

She winked at him. "Good thing you aren't. I'll be right back."

As she reached into her purse, she was reminded once again that she had to make her money last. She still had money in her account and small royalties trickling in, but this would almost finish out the cash she'd brought with her on the trip. She counted it out and fortunately came up with the exact amount.

"For your uh, services," she told him as she handed him the bills, making sure to brush his hand just a little.

He shot her a smoldering look. "Thanks. So, I don't guess I have to buy you lunch?"

She looked him right in the eye. "Well, I haven't seen him but not unless you just want to buy my lunch." She could tell her directness unnerved him just a bit and she relished the power.

Thankful for a distraction, he folded up the cash and put it in his wallet. "Let me know if you have any problems with his feet."

"And just how am I supposed to do that? Other than Susan, I don't know how to get in touch with you. In fact, I don't know anything about you."

He pulled out his business card and smiled as he handed it to her. "I don't know if I should give this to you or not."

"What? You're worried I might be calling you at all hours of the night?" She smiled sweetly as she took the card.

"Exactly. And then I'd have to endure seeing you naked again."

She blushed slightly and laughed. "Yeah, I don't think I could live through that again."

"Yeah, me neither."

She playfully punched him in the arm. "That's not very nice!"

"I'm just saying…"

"Get out of here and go shoe your other horses."

He turned to leave but stopped as he pulled the door knob. "There's a little diner in town that I go eat at most days during lunch. How about you meet me there tomorrow? Little place called Bill's. I'm sure you can find it with that GPS."

"I'll think about it. If I do, maybe that GPS can get me out of here."

He looked at the floor and shook his head. "I'll see you tomorrow."

When the door closed, Lily squealed to herself and took a little celebratory leap. Then she panicked, thinking he might have seen her through the kitchen window. Fortunately, his back was turned, and he didn't see a thing.

Chapter Three

By early afternoon Lily had finished unpacking all of her things and was settled in. She'd even managed to set up her internet and a little writing area in the front corner of the living room right under the window where she could look out at the green fields as she composed her next bestseller.

Thinking she really did need to try to get some writing in, she turned on her computer and sat down. All she could do however was stare at the blank screen. There were plenty of thoughts rolling around in her head but none of them had to do with writing. It seemed that writer's block had come to visit.

Instead she decided to check her email. She scanned through the long list of emails which were nothing but promotional junk mail. There were no emails from friends, family or readers.

"Well, that just sucks."

Suddenly the overwhelming feelings of loneliness that she had been keeping at bay for the last few months took over and the tears fell. She had no one. No one except a palomino gelding and a book agent who had just canned her book. How in the world did she ever get to this point?

Determined to change her mood, she focused on her latest curiosity, Carter Shelton. If he wasn't going to talk, she was going to do some research and find out what she wanted to know. There was a story there... and it might just be her next bestseller.

She typed "Carter Shelton, Willowcreek" in Google search and waited. She quickly scanned through the usual results until she saw a news link. Her pulse quickened as she clicked.

"Twenty-five years ago today marks the anniversary of the most devastating fire in Willowcreek history. The eight-hundred-acre fire not only changed the course of the town's future but also took the town's Mayor and well-known farmer, Sam Fischer. Fischer's neighbors Hank and Marie Shelton lost their lives to the fire as well, leaving behind an only son, Carter Shelton."

***

Lily scanned through the old pictures in the newspaper article looking for any sign of Carter, but she saw none. There were only pictures of burned buildings and firemen sifting through the charred rubble.

She clicked on the photo of Hank Shelton. A thin haggard man that Lily guessed to be in his fifties stared back at her. In his younger days, she imagined he would have looked a lot like Carter did now, but it was clearly evident that something had taken the spark out of him.

"There's a story here. I know it and I bet that's the reason he's so tight lipped about himself."

She spent the rest of the afternoon doing various versions of searches but found no more information on the enigma that was Hank Shelton and his son Carter.

***

Lily took another sip of her soft drink and looked at her phone again. It was 12:20 in the afternoon and Carter hadn't shown up. Although she really wanted to see him, there was a side of her that was getting a bit uncomfortable with all the glances from the farmers that walked in to the diner. She tried to pretend she was thoroughly engrossed in surfing on her phone but their curious looks managed to unsettle her tough exterior.

"Hun, you want some more Coke?"

"It's Dr. Pepper, and yes I'd like some more."

"You ain't from around here, are ya?"

Lily laughed. "No hun, I'm not."

Lily's comment wiped whatever Southern hospitality might have been on the young girl's face. "Well, everything is called coke around here."

"I see." Suddenly she remembered Carter. Surely if he came in here every day the young waitress would know what time he usually showed up. "Do you know Carter Shelton that shoes horses?"

The waitress laughed. "Let me guess, Carter asked you to meet him here?"

"Well, yes. What's so funny about that?"

"Let me put it to ya this way, hun," the waitress scoffed. "Carter meets a lot of clients here. You're just the flavor of the week."

Lily took a deep breath and reined in her emotions as she didn't want to give in to small town gossip usually started by waitresses just like this one. She knew that the little old local church ladies would have a field day if they heard she was after Carter, especially with her having been married five times and divorced. Although publicity was usually good for a book, she wanted to keep some dignity intact so she played it nonchalant. "I see. Well, what time does he normally show up?"

"About now. Won't be long. I'll go get you that Coke, I mean Dr. Pepper." She turned to go but then stopped and added, "And if I was you, I wouldn't put a whole lot of stock in getting attached to the likes of a cowboy like him. He's not the marryin' kind, if you know what I mean."

"Well who the hell said anything about marrying?" Lily snapped a little too loudly. Several farmers hushed their conversations and glanced up.

The waitress snickered and left for the kitchen.

As if right on cue, Carter Shelton breezed through the door of the small diner. Lily raised her arm to get his attention and he smiled back when he saw her. As he strode towards the little booth, Lily once again took in his long, tall frame. He sure did fill out a pair of wranglers, no doubt about it.

Not being one to play games, Lily got right to the point as he sat down. "So, I understand from the cute little waitress over there you meet quite a few clients here for lunch." She took a sip of her drink and casually glanced up at him to gage his reaction.

"Actually, I do. You know, a good farrier is in high demand these days." He flashed that grin that seemed to reach the deepest parts of her body.

"Is that a fact?"

He cocked his head to the side and said confidently, "Yes, it is."

Lily noticed his quick little glance at the opening of her shirt and wondered what she was doing here. If she kept following this path, she'd be in bed with him by the end of the week at the latest. Although the thought of being hot, sweaty and all tangled up in the sheets excited her, she quickly remembered where it got her the last time and decided to get her mind off such thoughts. "So, what's good to eat here?"

"Well, I kind of like their hamburgers. They get all their beef local and Bill back there does a good job of cookin' it up."

"There goes my diet, but it sure sounds good."

"Let me guess, you're a vegetarian?" He teased.

"Well, no but I do try to eat healthy when I can." And when she could afford it. But she didn't tell him that part.

"I'm going to eat whatever I feel like eatin'. I figure if it's my time to go, it's my time. It doesn't have a whole lot to do with if I decide to eat a hamburger or some tofu."

The waitress came to their table. "So Carter, what are you going to have today?"

"Well Maggie, what do I have every day?" he asked her as he pushed his cowboy hat back.

"Hamburger and fries," she replied as she squinted at him.

"Well, that's what I'm having."

"You don't have to be a smart ass about it."

"I'm not. But every day we have this same conversation."

"Yeah, that and me asking who you're meeting today." She looked at Lily and then smiled a sly smile.

Both ladies enjoyed the quick blush of color that showed up on Carter's cheeks. "Just get my hamburger. Maggie."

"And what do you want, ma'am?"

"I'll have the same thing he's having." Lily watched as Maggie wrote her order and left for the kitchen.

"So, how's your horse this morning? Is he moving out alright?" he asked as he leaned back against the booth.

"He's actually doing fine."

"So, you buying my dinner?"

She stiffened. "Wait a minute! You didn't say anything about me buying your dinner if I was pleased with your shoeing."

"Well, I was willing to buy yours if you weren't happy," he teased.

"You just invited me here to get a free dinner?" Lily asked.

"Wasn't that the reason you were considering coming to begin with?"

His devilish grin caught her off guard, again. "Well, yes, but…"

"What's the difference?"

"I thought this was the South where men were gentleman." She offered.

Carter leaned forward and winked. "I never said I was a gentleman."

"Well, you definitely never said that," she agreed.

"I don't really see you as the type that would fancy a gentleman." Carter laughed softly and sat back to enjoy the crimson making its way up her cheeks. "I don't buy lunch for just anyone, but I figure since you moved into Susan's place you could probably use a free meal. Only one type of woman moves into that place."

While she was relieved she wouldn't have to buy both their lunches, she was mortified at the fact that he pegged her taste in men and at the same time she was offended at his assessment of her predicament. "Just what type is that?"

"The type that's down on their luck," he told her.

"You think I'm down on my luck? That I can't make it on my own?" She chewed on her bottom lip to fight back the tears that were suddenly burning her eyes.

Carter shook his head. One thing he hated was to see a woman cry. "Do you barrel race? I mean, when you're not writing books or chasing your farrier around naked."

Lily was thankful for the quick change of subject, and the devilish gleam in his eye. "Yes, as a matter of fact I do. Barrel race, that is. I only chase farriers naked if they deserve it." Tears suddenly gone, she met his gaze head on and sipped deliberately through the straw in her drink.

"Well, I can't quite imagine what I did to deserve such poor treatment as that," he taunted.

"Carter Shelton, you are one rude individual," she countered.

"I'm buying you lunch, aren't I?"

"Well, yes, but…"

"And your horse is moving fine, isn't he?"

"Yes…"

"Well, then why are you calling me rude?" He crossed his arms and sat back in the booth and enjoyed watching her squirm.

"I… well, you…"

"The great writer doesn't have anything to say?" he gloated.

"Dammit!"

"That's harsh language coming from someone looking for a Southern gentleman."

"I never said I wanted one."

Right about then Lily wished she had a stiff drink instead of a Dr. Pepper. Carter's smoldering look was a bit too much for her to handle and made her squirm. Fortunately, Maggie showed up with two large plates of food.

"Can I get y'all anything else?"

Unable to look up, Lily just shook her head.

"Well, I'm afraid our writer here is a bit speechless."

"Carter, just leave her alone," she chided. She gave Lily a sympathetic look, "Let me know if you need anything."

"There's a barrel race with added money next weekend up at Ellis State Expo Center. It's about an hour haul from here. Might be a good place to take that yellow horse of yours."

Glad for the abrupt change of subject, Lily finally managed to eke out a weak "Maybe so."

"Well, I mean you don't have to, but I just thought you might want to get out since you're new around here and all." In the midst of a big bite of hamburger he added, "I can get you a ride if you need one."

"Didn't anyone ever tell you not to talk with your mouth full?" She caught the slight rush of color that made its way up his cheeks as he shook his head. "I can haul myself. Last time I hauled with someone else it didn't go so well."

Carter quickly finished the big bite of sandwich he was working on. "What happened?"

"I came back to the tack room to find my hauling partner making out with my ex-husband."

"Ouch. Wasn't quite expecting that answer! Figured it was more along the lines of she was always bitchin' about something."

"I wish. She was my best friend too. She was a career moocher and had been telling me about this wonderful new mystery guy that was bank rolling her barrel racing. Turns out it was my husband."

"What did you do?" he asked a little too eagerly.

Lily chuckled. "I can tell you're not one to miss out on a cat fight, are you?"

"Well, I mean the story is pretty good!"

"I felt like grabbing her by the back of the head and slamming it into the edge of the gooseneck, but I figured neither one of them were worth the effort, so I divorced his ass."

"And to think you missed out on an opportunity to let go of some steam."

"Well, looking back I should have gotten at least some satisfaction out of it. He took me to the cleaners in the divorce." She shook her head. "I should have known better."

"And that's how you ended up at Susan's?"

"Yep. Pretty much."

"Ok, spill the rest of it. Don't tell me you're wanted for public indecency."

"No, although that might be a bit more interesting than the real reason."

"And?"

Once again, his close scrutiny was making her a bit uncomfortable yet for some reason his full attention made her want to divulge more than she knew she should. "Okay fine. I'll tell you. The publisher canned my latest book."

"And you came here looking for a new start and a new story. Is that it?" He leaned in and studied her even closer.

How did he know her so well? "Yep, that's it," she said as she took a big bite of fries.

"So how likely am I to end up in one of your romances?"

She had to admit, his smile was infectious and those dark eyes she could get lost in, but she wouldn't let him win out that easy. "You have to be damn good to get into one my romances, cowboy. I didn't get on the bestsellers list by writing about wannabes."

"I don't believe in romance anyhow," he scoffed.

"Neither do I, but that doesn't mean that I can't write about it…especially with a little inspiration." She cast a sly glance in his direction as she sipped on the rest of her drink.

Suddenly she remembered the article online and couldn't fight the urge to ask. "Speaking of stories, what's the scoop behind the fire that broke out years ago here in town?"

Carter sputtered out Coke and fries before finally managing to gather his wits. "Where the hell did you find out about the fire? From Susan?" he hissed angrily. Once again, the farmers glanced up at the farrier they knew a little too well in the booth, their curiosity peaking.

Lily lowered her voice. "No, I didn't."

"I guess you read about it online?" he sneered back in a quieter tone.

Lily was confused by his abrupt change in demeanor. "Yes, in fact I did."

"I guess because you read it online you think it's true."

"Well Carter, did it happen or not?"

He clenched his jaw. "Yes, it happened."

"Then what are you so upset about? It's not like you set it or anything." Lily watched as the color drained from his face.

"It happened years ago and quite frankly that fire ruined this town…and my whole world. This is something I'm not going to talk about, especially with you."

"Look Carter, I didn't mean to hit a nerve," she apologized. "I was just asking." Suddenly she felt bad for letting her inner curiosity monster out. Yet, at the same time she couldn't help but wonder why the topic made him so angry. She was sure it had devastated this small town in a lot of ways, but was that really a reason to get so angry at the mere mention of the event?

At that, they ate in silence for a few moments, each wondering what the other was thinking, until Maggie came by to see if they needed anything as she dropped off the check. They both reached for the green and white slip of paper at the same time, locked in an electric tug of war as their skin touched.

"I've got it," Carter said.

"No, I'll get it. I don't want you to feel sorry for me."

He shook his head. "I don't feel sorry for you. I just said I'll get it."

She kept her grip. "Well, if you don't feel sorry for me, then why do you want to pay the bill?" It was an honest question.

"Maybe… I don't know…. Just let me pay the damn ticket," he said as he jerked it away from her hot grip.

"Fine," she pouted. But inside her heart was still racing at the mere touch of his hand. She had to get grip on herself.

"You could at least say, 'Thank you'. Or did they not teach you that out there in Texas?"

"Thank you," she said coldly.

"I'm sure you'll find a way to make it up to me," he teased.

As she waited for him to pay at the register, she quietly stood back and admired the view while she took note. She'd known a lot of men in her life, too many in fact, but there was something about Carter Shelton that drew her in. Something more than a nicely filled out pair of wranglers, a rugged jaw or a boyish grin. One minute he was a jerk and the next moment she was getting a slight glimpse of some manners.

Maybe it was the challenge of not knowing anything about him? She wasn't sure, but it was obvious that Maggie was under the same spell as she giggled a little too loudly at something Carter said. She'd wanted to hit Maggie up for more information. Of course, she knew she couldn't as any interest in Carter Shelton would spread around this small town faster than the great fire she'd read about, especially interest from a well-known author with a less than spectacular relationship history.

Carter held the door open for her as they headed outside and for the first time in a long time, she let him. "Thanks."

"So, you never said if you were going to the barrel race or not."

"I might," she offered.

"You should. I'd like to see you run."

"Why? So you can critique me?" she asked hopefully.

"Nope. So I can see how well those shoes work," he retorted.

"Oh. Well, I'll think about it," she said as she nervously dug the toe of her boot into a few pebbles on the sidewalk. Once again, he'd let the air out of her sails just as she hoped there might be some real interest on his behalf.

"You do that." He winked and walked off to his truck on the other side of the street.

"Hey, how do I find where the barrel race is?" she called out to him.

"Oh, I'm sure you can find Ellis State Expo in that little GPS of yours," he said as he shut the door to his truck and turned on the engine.

Lily shook her head and walked to her truck, smiling and yet a bit confused about his abruptness in leaving. Somewhere in the back of her mind she'd fantasized about him having a lingering conversation with her. So much for those romantic fairy tales she often wrote about.

Chapter Four

Lily tightened up her cinch one last time and then pulled her stirrup fender down. She'd given Mercado a few extra days to settle in to his new home and his new shoes. She was more than ready to go check out the miles of trails Susan had told her were on the back side of the farm.

A lifelong cowgirl, Lily could never find it within herself to go without riding for more than just a couple of days at a time. Even if it meant throwing a leg over a horse bareback, she had to get a ride in or the world would start to close in on her. Riding was her sanity in a crazy world.

Just as she put a foot in her stirrup, she felt her phone buzz in the holder on her belt. She stopped and pulled her phone out to see who it could be – being a starving author that needed a new gig, she couldn't afford to distance herself from the only line to civilization.

How's the book coming along?

"Why is he texting me on a Saturday afternoon asking me how the book is coming along?" She said it to no one in particular except maybe Mercado whose ears twitched back and forth.

She debated whether or not she should tell him the truth. She decided to fudge it a little. Well, a lot actually.

Great. I already have a story idea.

Instead of stepping up into the saddle, she waited for Nate's response.

I look forward to reading it. When do you think you'll be done?

"Good Lord, Nate, you never pushed this much on my best sellers. I wonder what's up…"

Not sure. Heading out to do research. I'll give you an update later. Hugs.

"That will have to do for now, Nate," she told her phone.

As usual, she had already wasted half the day. She was ready to get out and explore for the rest of the afternoon.

Grabbing the rein in the left hand, she stuck her foot in the stirrup and boosted herself up. Once in the saddle, she found the other stirrup and reined the quiet palomino towards the sage covered ridge on the other side of the road.

The view from the top of the hill was more than she had expected. One of the highest places in the valley, everywhere she looked was either rolling green pasture or thick woods. Definitely a lot greener than the brown Southwest.

Off to the right, tucked in a small hollow at the edge of the woods, stood a farm house with a wraparound porch. Right behind the house was a big red barn surrounded by an old black creosote fence that was falling down. From the location Lily guessed it was Susan's house.

She knew that if she took a left that she would eventually wind up at the main road. She wanted to explore somewhere new and thus headed straight ahead.

The grass was so thick and tall that Lily couldn't see the ground beneath. Although his head was up and his ears forward on alert, the palomino slowly picked his way through without any spooking or stumbling.

At the bottom of the hill, Lily saw the faint trace of a dirt cattle trail leading off through the tall sage. She decided to pick up the path to find out where it led.

Now able to see the ground a little better, Lily bumped Mercado into a nice long trot and started posting. As the pathway ambled back and forth over the now rocky and uneven ground, Lily was glad the gelding had a good handle. It was a bit of a challenge keeping the pace and staying on the narrow stretch of bare ground.

The pair followed the pathway around a small rise and suddenly Mercado stopped. At the edge of the tree line a little way off, were three black cows that suddenly jerked their heads up and took off in the opposite direction.

Although Mercado had seen cattle before, apparently it wasn't on a green background. With one abrupt leap, the palomino gelding darted left and bolted in the opposite direction of the cows. Lily pitched back hard and sideways. In desperation, she scrambled to regain her balance and grab the saddle horn and reins, but it was too late. Already at a full gallop, she shut her eyes against the green blur getting ever closer and tucked hard for the brutal impact that was about to hit.

Her shoulder and then her head struck the hard ground. A burst of bright, multi-colored lights filled her sight. Although both body parts hurt tremendously, it was the hard lump in her chest that felt the worst. It was as if Mercado himself had kicked her square in the chest and her lungs were too heavy to lift. She pushed at the pain with everything she had.

The air wasn't coming. She had to get up. Fighting back the tears, she pushed herself over on her side. Then she managed to get up on her knees where she bent over in another attempt to breathe. The lack of oxygen was frightening, and in a panic, she saw herself dying in this very field.

In frustration and fear, she pounded the ground with her fists and screamed with everything she had. Suddenly the air rushed into her lungs, bringing the dam of tears with it.

She sat back in the tall green grass and watched as Mercado disappeared over the next hill. She looked down at her legs and arms to take an assessment of whether not anything was broken. She moved each one of her legs, and although her hind end was awfully sore from the impact, it didn't feel as though anything was out of place. The only real injury was a decent scrape on her forearm. Being that she wasn't a spring chicken anymore, she knew she was lucky and quite honestly it was her pride that was hurt most of all. It was time to hit the core work a little harder so this wouldn't happen again.

With a lot of effort and wincing, she stood up and headed in the direction that her fleet footed gelding had headed. She hoped that he would be over the next ridge, but the grass was green and she was a long way from Texas. So far it was evident that anything was possible.

She worked up a sweat as she walked, which of course also attracted tiny black gnats and mosquitoes. They crowded her eyes and nose with a frenzy, and in the process she managed to accidently slap herself several times in an attempt to cease the buzzing that was now driving her insane. She had to find that horse and get out of there!

As she topped the ridge, she saw her gelding calming grazing in a patch of dark green clover. Although she had quite a hike to get him, she was relieved to see him standing still in a place she could get to. Then something else caught her eye just to the right.

Black charred pieces of wood and stone stood out against the backdrop of green and golden sage that surrounded it. It was as though time had collided. A piece of history mixed with new growth that had taken over, a vivid metaphor of life right before her very eyes.

Lily walked in the direction where Mercado was grazing, all the while scanning the ruins of a forgotten life before her. She was mesmerized by the possibility of what she might find in the charred ruins.

Her imagination ran rampant with all kinds of crazy ideas. A souvenir of a discarded past? Perhaps a hoard of treasure, or...maybe the answer to the Willowcreek fire all those years ago?

She was a long way from town and from what little she had read, she got the impression that fire had started just a few miles away. Then again, there was still a lot she didn't know about the fire, but Carter's reaction had made her want to know more.

Lily hurried in anticipation of getting a closer look. When she finally reached Mercado, he was still standing in the same place making quick work of the tender white bloomed clover. Against all odds, her leather reins were still intact. She grabbed for the end and with a little effort brought Mercado's head up from the buffet and looped her reins around the limb of a nearby tree. Then she turned her attention toward the pile of rubble down below.

Lily walked the border of the tangled mass of charred wood and grown up vegetation looking for any clues that would tell her about this place and what had happened here. She felt the urge to tear through the thick dark green vines and reveal the mystery underneath, but the thought of snakes kept her from it. She had an unnatural fear of snakes, which was one of the reasons she didn't even own a pair of snakeskin boots.

Whatever the building used to be, Lily could tell that it was big and had burned hot enough to disintegrate most of the wood. If not for a stark black random beam here and there that had drawn her eye, she would have never seen the remains through the ivy and vegetation.

The question of what happened here drew her in like a moth to a flame. Snakes or not, she couldn't fight the urge to at least dig through the weeds to a large beam jutting out from a young willow tree that had taken root.

Taking extra care that her feet were safe from any slithering reptiles, Lily grabbed the edge of the charred wood and lifted. The wood moved back easily, revealing beneath it a rough-hewn patchwork of hardwood boards. Between the crevices of where the boards went together was a fine mix of yellow straw and sawdust.

"This must have been a barn," Lily said to no one in particular as Mercado was still several feet away and now dozing in the shade.

Encouraged to find pieces of the past, she tugged on the boards, dragging them away from the ivy that held on as though not to give up its secrets. Underneath, stuck to the damp clay, lay the torn remains of a flower print cloth edged in lace. Lily traced the old lace with her finger.

Stretching precariously over the tall briars, she reached as far as she could and grabbed a handful of the cloth and lifted it up. As she felt for the edge of the cloth, her hand bumped against a small piece of metal. She grasped the edge of it with the tips of her fingers and tugged. It gave a little, then got stuck. Whatever the object was, it was attached to something.

Suddenly something let go, sending Lily face first into the dirt.

Sputtering earth and curse words out between her teeth, she jerked herself up off the damp ground and scrambled to her feet as she looked around for a snake that she just knew had to be somewhere close.

"Just my luck…"

She looked down at the encrusted metal piece still in her grip and ran her fingers over the rough dirt-encased edge. It was the shape of a long antique key attached to a chain. She held it up to the dim afternoon light.

"Well, I wonder what this little gem went to." She turned it over in her hands and looked for any sign of writing.

She suspected this place and the key was somehow tied to the fire in town, but it was anyone's guess as Carter refused to talk.

"I think I might have to pay Susan a visit to find out what all this is about."

She glanced at the afternoon sun just over the ridge. The sun was setting fast and she needed to get back before dark.

Chapter Five

Lily was bent over and lost in her own little world of calculating whether the store brand of chili was actually cheaper than the name brand when she felt a buggy bump up hard against her hips.

"Hey... Damnit!" she snapped as she wheeled around to see what asshole had just bumped into her. She met Carter's infectious grin.

"Well, ya know it was sticking out there in the way." He tipped his worn hat back on his head and continued, "And it was kind of hard to miss."

"Carter Shelton, how dare you!" Lily hissed, although her hot anger was quickly turning to something else.

"I see your little GPS got you to town."

Lily rolled her eyes and laughed. "Now I just need it to tell me how to cook on a budget."

Carter glanced down at the sparse buggy with a few canned items. "Just what are you trying to cook?" he asked.

"Anything good and cheap."

Before he knew it, the words just slipped out. "How about I get us a couple of steaks and we'll cook out at your place. Susan's got an old grill on that back porch."

"Let me guess, you used that with your last fling that rented there?" She watched the color creep up his face.

"Ok, you caught me," he admitted. "Doesn't mean we can't have a good supper."

Lily glanced down at her boots to avoid Carter's intense gaze. Why did this have to happen? It was much simpler when she was chasing.

On the one hand, she wanted nothing more than to spend some time with Carter, but on the other, she was trying hard to mend her ways and the last thing she wanted to do was fall hard and wind up in bed with another cowboy that would break her heart – and she knew Carter would do just that. He did draw her in… and it was a free dinner.

"Alright," she told him as she scuffed the edge of her boot against the floor. She would have to stay on her guard.

"C'mon, let's go pick out some steaks. Just put your stuff in my cart. No sense in pushing two of these things around the store." He dropped the cans in his cart, and then grabbed her hand, pulling her with him.

That ambiguous territory of holding hands, the first step of showing interest. It could mean just that or something more. It was exciting, yet the big question loomed even larger as he rubbed his thumb against the back side of her hand. Where was this going?

Her body tingled with the unexpected excitement of his enormous hand around hers. She wasn't a tiny girl by any means, but his fingers dwarfed hers as he laced her hand with his and held it close.

Although her libido was already on high alert, that one simple gesture had her feeling emotions she didn't know how to handle. She didn't feel alone, but she also felt protected and safe and that was something she wasn't expecting.

"What are you grinning for? You look like a big possum," he teased as he pulled her to the back of the store.

Lily playfully punched him in the arm. "That little analogy wasn't nice!"

"I never claimed to be nice." He winked, then squeezed her hand.

A little shock went through her body, but she played it cool, "You are correct about that."

"T-bones or ribeye?" he asked.

"Ribeye."

"Good choice," he said as he released his grip, then grabbed two steaks and put them in the cart.

Her hand felt naked without his warm grasp around it. She wondered if he would grab her hand again, or if his actions had just been a fleeting thought.

"What else do you want to go with the steaks? Potatoes and salad?"

She liked the way he had stepped in and took control without being too pushy. It had been a long time since she could relax and go along for the ride. "Sounds good."

This time, Carter didn't reach for her hand as they headed for the produce section. Still high off of the feel of her hand in his, but yet not wanting to get her hopes up, Lily distanced herself just a little. She didn't want to seem mad, but at the same time she didn't want to read too much into his actions or be too clingy. Why did this have to be so complicated?

"Need anything else?" he asked her as he picked up a head of lettuce and some colored peppers.

"Well, I do need to finish getting the rest of my groceries for the week since I'm in town. Toilet paper, shampoo, that sort of thing."

"That's fine. I don't have anywhere I have to be."

Lily felt a little odd as he followed her around the store with the shopping cart and waited patiently as she chose items off the shelves. It almost felt as though they were comfortable with the each other, like an old couple that had been together for years, but they had just met.

As they stepped in line at the checkout, Lily separated out her groceries from the steaks and salad.

"What are you doing?" Carter asked.

"Pulling my stuff to the side."

"Leave it. I've got it."

"Carter, no. I can't let you do that. I'll get it. I didn't take you up on your offer so you could buy my groceries."

"I know that." He took the can from her. "I said I've got it, now let me get it."

She looked into his dark eyes that were now just a little too serious. She wasn't sure how far she could push. On one hand it would help her not to have to pay for groceries for a week, but was it worth the cost of his thinking that she needed help?

Even through five divorces she'd always managed to support herself through her writing, no matter what. This was the first time in her entire life she'd questioned her ability to support herself financially.

As though sensing the turmoil in her head, Carter said, "I know you can take care of yourself. Just let me get it, ok?"

Lily nodded yes and stood there in silence as the cashier ran the items through the scanner.

Carter didn't miss the slight look of relief on Lily's face when he said he'd pay. He wasn't sure how Lily had wound up in this small nowhere town all the way from west Texas, but he was pretty sure it wasn't because she'd picked out the most desirable town to come to. He knew that most likely, just like Susan's other residents, it was because she was down on her luck and she needed a place to fall.

Susan's place was cheap, but it was also bare bones. No one ever rented there unless they were desperate. He figured Lily was desperate too, he just didn't know why. That part intrigued him, especially since she was like a cat - he'd figured out pretty quick that she always landed on her feet. What was she doing at Susan's?

***

The whole way back to the house, Lily was replaying Carter's actions in the grocery store and trying to figure out what her next move needed to be. Any other time, she would have him in bed by the end of the night. After all, a pair of wranglers that fit just right had that kind of effect on a woman. But she'd been down that road far too many times, and look where it got her – broke, and alone. No, this time, if there was going to be a "this time", she wanted something more. Something much more.

Wait a minute. What did she want? What was this thing with Carter all about? Hadn't she come here to find herself, find her muse and write a new book that was a bestseller? That's what she had to do if she was going to pull herself out of this black hole that she'd gotten herself into. Carter wasn't a part of that.

He was good looking and had a magnetic personality, no doubt about that. He was also a distraction that really had no part in what she needed to do.

In the end, the question she asked herself was whether or not she could get close to the fire and not get pulled in? She had to stay focused on writing her story and maybe winning a few barrel races if she could.

***

Carter closed his eyes as he chewed a juicy piece of grilled ribeye. "Hmmm. Now, that's a steak."

Lily enjoyed his reaction and then re-directed the thought that wondered if he looked like that every time he was satisfied.

"I take it I did a good job on the steak and the marinade?"

"Yes, you did." He smiled at her as he took another bite.

"I'm glad you like it." She was genuinely pleased that he was enjoying her cooking.

"Yep, you did a fine job."

"Well, you know I hear Texas is all about the beef."

"That's what I hear. Speaking of Texas, how did a woman like you wind up in Tennessee?" He grinned and looked her dead in the eyes as he took another juicy bite of meat.

His abrupt question and intense attention caught her off guard. At this point she wasn't sure she really wanted to tell him everything. On the one hand, he might run – which is exactly what she needed – but on the other that might just break her heart.

She chopped up her salad, which of course required all of her attention. Then she asked, "Do you really want me to tell you that ol' story and ruin what's been a great evening so far?"

"Yes, I'm curious." He reached over and tilted her chin up so she had to look at him. "Why here? Why Willowcreek of all places when you could have gone somewhere else? I mean, you're a bestselling author."

Suddenly the color drained from her face. How in the world did he know she was a bestselling author? She had only told him her name, not the fact that she'd been on the New York Times list more than once.

How could she tell him her latest book was a piece of crap, that she'd been divorced five times, and that she was down to her last penny?

"Research, I guess," she told him as she casually pulled away and took a long sip of red wine.

"Research? You move all the way out here to this little hole in the wall joint to do research? I don't buy it. What's the real story, Lily? What are you running from?"

He'd watched her squirm before, and quite honestly had enjoyed it, but this time was different. He saw that same sadness he'd gotten a glimpse of at the diner and it stirred something deep within him. Most of the time a woman's tears didn't bother him one bit – Lord only knew he'd made enough women cry in his time. Lily was different. He wanted to know what it was that lay beneath that fiery exterior that had driven her to come all the way across the country by herself.

He reached over and pushed soft, curly strands of red hair back from her face and stared into the prettiest green eyes he was sure he'd ever seen. Except now those eyes were brimming with tears and for some strange reason he felt the need to kiss them away.

Without saying a word, he leaned over and gently kissed Lily on the forehead. "I want to know, but not because of the reason you think I do." He told her as he pressed his forehead against hers and then pulled back when he realized what he'd done.

Lily stared at him, gauging his deep, dark brown eyes for any sign that he was playing her. This was a side she hadn't seen of Carter, and she didn't know what to expect. Was this all just a ploy to get her in bed, or did he really care on some level? It was so hard to tell!

"Why do you want to know, Carter? Is it because you want me to think you care so that you can get me in bed? Or is it that you're truly interested?" She intently watched his face, looking for any crack in what could be a ruse.

"I'm truly interested. I know you don't think so. Can't say I blame you for thinking that way, considering my reputation."

"And just what reputation is that?" She grinned slyly as she sat back and took another sip of wine.

"Being somewhat of a lady's man, I guess. Comes with the territory of being a farrier." He chuckled.

"Tell me why I would tell you all my secrets?"

"Didn't ask for your secrets, just what you were running from."

"Damnit, Carter. What the hell am I supposed to do with that?"

"This." He pulled her to him and burned his lips upon hers as his teeth gently tugged at her lower lip.

She nipped back and sucked at his lip that was now between hers. It was as if time stood still, and her body was consumed by the fire he ignited that burned through her loins. She couldn't think, she couldn't breathe...and that was just one kiss.

Carter pulled his mouth away from hers and nuzzled her ear and neck, sending shivers throughout her body. She let out a little groan and dug her fingers into his wavy dark hair.

Stoking a fire in the likes of a woman such as Lily surely fueled his ego, and his desire. He enjoyed having that effect on a woman. Although he was most definitely enjoying her reaction and wanted nothing more than to take her to bed, something stopped him cold. He wasn't sure if it was because she had his number on being a womanizer, or if it was something more.

He stroked the mass of curls and kissed the top of her head. "I want this just as much as you do Lily, but not tonight. Not this soon, and not like this."

"What..." She looked up at him with eyes that held a mix of hurt and fiery anger.

He held her back away from him. "I don't want to hurt you, and I don't want to get hurt either."

She pulled away from his grip. "Carter, I don't know what game you're playing. One minute you're hot, and I'm hot. The next minute you're as cold as ice."

"I don't know how to deal with you either! You're not like any woman I've ever met, Lily, and I don't know what to do with that."

She chuckled. "Of course I'm not like any woman you've ever met, especially in this place! I could think of quite a few things you could do, and normally, I would be up for that but I'm tired of getting hurt and I'm tired of being used. I want something more. I don't know what that is necessarily. I'm not giving myself up that easily anymore."

He grabbed her around the waist and brought her firm against him so that he felt the full length of her body.

"Not even for someone like me?" He gave her a devilish grin and then nuzzled her neck before placing a firm kiss just below her left ear.

Lily let out a little groan and then pushed back away from him. "Especially not for someone like you!"

"What do we do?" he asked, trapping her once again in his strong arms.

Lily rested her hands on his arms, taking close note of the firm defined bicep just below his shirt. Even just considering something with the likes of Carter Shelton was dangerous. He was just the right mix of confident cowboy with a tender edge that showed up only once in a while.

"I'm not sure." She sighed. "I don't need entanglements, but I don't want casual sex either."

"Wow, just say it like it is," he half-laughed and turned her loose.

"You wouldn't expect anything less," she told him.

"No...I have to admit you're right about that."

"Look, I'm not like you. I don't live in the small town I grew up in where everyone knows me, and everyone has my back if I need it. It's just me and I'm on my own."

"No family?" he asked.

"Nope, both parents are dead."

"No brothers or sisters?"

"Half-brother, but I don't even know where he is or if he's even still alive."

"Cousins?"

"I never knew them."

"What are you doing here?"

"Oh Carter..."

"Are you wanted by the law or something?"

Lily shook her head.

"That's it! You're wanted for bank robbery! I knew it. You're just keeping it low key while you're hiding," he teased unmercifully.

"No." She put her hands on her hips.

He pointed at her abandoned plate sitting on the edge of the table. "Better finish your steak before it gets cold."

She grabbed her plate and took a bite, and then said, "If you want to know, I'll tell you, but you've got to promise me you won't make any smart remarks."

She wanted him to tell him everything, although she wasn't sure why. Maybe because she was lonely and had no one, but she knew she would run the risk of his judgement and alienation – and then where would she be? Susan was the only person she knew in this part of the country. Which, now that she thought about it, was pretty sad considering she'd been a bestselling author.

"I promise," he said with a smile that didn't match his words.

"I mean it! Not one smart comment."

"Okay! Spill it."

"Alright." She took a deep sigh and then a long sip of wine. "I haven't sold a decent story in over a year. My agent, Nate, called and told me that my publisher canned my latest story after we'd signed a contract." She took another drink. "And, I've just lost everything but what you see here in a nasty divorce from husband number five. I needed a cheap place to start over and find my muse."

She held her breath as she waited for Carter to respond.

"Husband number five?"

It was not the response she was expecting. "Ouch. Yes, number five. I told you I was tired of relationships."

"I guess I can understand why."

She scowled at him. "Look, you asked why I was here and I told you. I didn't ask you to judge me." She should have known better than to tell him the truth, let alone agree to dinner at her place. She suspected this was the last time that she would see him outside of shoeing Mercado. "It's getting late." She got up and sat her plate on the counter.

"It's only 7pm." He reached and grabbed her arm but she shrugged away.

"Well, I'm sure you've got to be somewhere early in the morning. Besides, I've got a few things I have to do myself."

"If that's what you want." He put his plate in the sink. "So I guess you're mad at me now." He searched her face for any sign of what she was thinking but it was obvious she'd pulled her feelings behind the walls that she'd built up.

"No, I'm not mad. Hurt maybe, but I'll get over it. I am what I am, people either take it or leave it. There's no in between. You can't help it if you can't see past what I've told you already. Not many can and that's ok. It is what it is. I deal with it."

"Lily…" Something deep down stirred within him and he hurt for her, but he was at a complete loss for words.

"Don't. It's okay. I'm fine. I'm assuming you know your way out."

"Alright. Well, I did have a nice time tonight." He didn't know what else to say.

"Me too. Thanks for the meal."

He nodded and started to say something but decided better of it and walked out the door to his truck. He needed to get away from this place as soon as possible.

Chapter Six

After Carter left, Lily busied herself with washing the dirty dishes, replaying in her head every single detail of what had happened. She could kick herself for telling him the truth, but then when had she ever told anything but the truth? She didn't know any other way to be and she'd always been the "what you see is what you get" type of girl. She had no reason to change that now, and maybe in this case it had saved her a lot of heartache.

Men were such funny creatures. You could show them all the ugliness from the beginning to which they responded they could most assuredly deal with it, only to slink off later because it was more than they'd bargained for. At least this time maybe she'd saved herself that hurt.

The more she thought about it, the more she realized it was better for both of them to walk away now. After five marriages, she knew she would be the gossip of the town anyway, especially if they got together. Not only that, she knew in the long run this small town would never satisfy her for very long, and Carter's roots went too deep to ever leave. It was just a heartache and misery waiting to happen and she didn't want any part of it.

Suddenly she heard her phone buzz. It was a message from Nate.

How's the book coming along?

She smiled. Nate had always been her biggest fan since she'd sold her first book to Crystal Publishing. From the very beginning, he'd taken a vested interest in writing, saw her potential, and pushed her further than she'd ever written before. This time he had been brutally honest, but she knew it was because he only wanted to see her succeed. He always had.

She lied. *Still working on my outline.*

A response came back instantly.

Can you tell me what it's about?

He was still pushing, even with the book cancellation.

Although she didn't have a solid plot, she had ironed out the fact that the book was going to take place in a small town and somehow involve the fire that she had accidently learned about. Now, how that was going to turn into a romance, she didn't have any idea. But it was a start.

Fire in a small town, lots of secrets.

There, that should satisfy him for now – she hoped.

Her phone rang. It was Nate.

She winced as she answered. "Hey. You must not have liked my story idea."

"How much have you actually written?"

She bit her lip. Truth or white lie?

"None. Still trying to iron out the details. I mean, I have the idea for the story, but I haven't developed my plot or created any characters. I'm working on it. Why are you pushing so hard? I figure you would be working on some other great writer's story since I can't write worth a damn."

"I never said that, Lil, I just said your story was crap. Look, I may have talked them into offering you another limited contract."

"Oh…"

"Yes, if you can get me three good chapters and a synopsis by the end of the month, they might consider signing on another book. That's three weeks away."

She took a drink. She didn't have a solid book plot at this point, just an idea. She'd never been one to write quickly and all her books had taken months, sometimes even a year to write. Three weeks was nothing to write a synopsis and three chapters and have them perfect.

"Three weeks?"

He heard the hesitation in her voice. "Yes, and I'll even offer to edit and proof it on my own time to make sure it's right."

"Isn't that conflict of interest?"

"Yes, but I know you need this."

"Why do you have to be taken? You're always so good to me."

He sighed. "You deserve it, Lil. You cut yourself short. You're a great writer, even if you do get sidetracked sometimes."

"I've got to do some research, but I guess it's sink or swim, right?"

"Pretty much. I've put my neck on the line this time and went to bat for you, so you've got to come through."

"I won't let you down."

"Tell you what, get your research done but send me final outline and character analysis by this Friday. I think we can pull it off if you stick to a hard schedule. You just need to be disciplined. You think you can do that? I'll help you with setting your deadlines."

"Yes, drill sergeant."

"You know you need me."

"In more ways than one." The words had come out easier than she'd anticipated, and she heard him cough on the line. "Cat got your tongue there, handsome?"

"Just get your outline done. I'll talk to you in a day or so. End of the week." He hung up.

Even after all these years, she'd never met Nate in person. When the publisher had flown her to New York for special events, they missed each other. One of these days she was going to have to make it a point to meet. She owed him a lot.

For the first time in weeks, she set her alarm. She would talk to Susan first thing in the morning now that she was committed to doing the research for the book. Maybe

Susan could shed some light on what had happened on the farm next door and perhaps help give her some direction for her story.

***

At eight in the morning, Lily stepped up on the gray wooden porch lined in large green ferns. It looked like a scene straight out of *Southern Living* with its white wicker furniture and white trim. She pushed the button on the large ornate copper doorbell and listened as the high-pitched chime rang.

She waited, noticing the large black ceiling fans placed every few feet down the large expansive front porch that ended with a white wooden swing. She imagined women with lace fans sitting around sipping sweet tea and gossiping in the heat of the afternoon.

Suddenly the screen door opened and Susan motioned her inside.

"Haven't had my coffee yet, so I'm not too sociable." She winked. "You want coffee?"

"Yes, if you have some. I apologize this was on such short notice."

"Don't worry. Truth be told, I'm up pretty early. Old habits die hard."

"What do you mean?" She followed Susan, who was still dressed in an old faded tee shirt and loose pajama bottoms to the kitchen.

"Dairyin'. Too many years milking cows and feeding stock." She gave a half smile as she poured a cup of coffee and handed it to Lily. "You need creamer?"

Lily nodded and watched the older woman grab the creamer from the fridge.

"So, what is it that you want to talk about on such short notice? Is everything okay down there? I saw Carter's truck there when I came through last night."

Lily blushed slightly at the mention of Carter's vehicle. True to form, there wasn't anything missed in a small town. She'd have to remember that if she didn't stay with her original plan of staying single.

"Oh, everything is going great. Mercado has settled in and we're both very happy there."

Susan smiled. "I'm glad. I know it can be hard being on your own as a woman sometimes, especially when things get a little tough. It's nice to have a soft place to fall."

She took a sip of coffee. It was hot and strong. "Good coffee. Actually, what I wanted to talk to you about is some research that I'm doing for a book that I'm working on."

"Oh...what kind of research?"

"The fire that took place here twenty or so years ago. I'm wondering if it had anything to do with the place that burned that's over the hill."

The color drained from Susan's face and Lily took note. There was a story here. She was sure of it, but she had to sweeten the deal just a bit as it seemed people didn't want to talk much about it.

"I'm working on a new story idea, a romance that takes place in a small town. My publisher has made an offer if I can get them a sample in a few weeks – I really need it since they canned my last book."

"What does the fire have to do with your book?" Susan asked as she settled back against the marble kitchen counter.

"Well, I'm not sure. I thought maybe if I could find out a little about how it started and the story behind it, I might get some ideas for the plot."

Susan sighed and looked up at her. "I don't know if that's a good idea, Lily."

"I'm not using any real people or events. I just thought finding out about it might be inspirational."

"Small town people are funny, Lily. We don't like to talk, especially to strangers."

"Well, they don't want to talk but they sure want to know about everyone else's business." The words just slipped out.

Susan laughed. "That's true."

"I'm sorry, I didn't mean…"

"No, you're speaking the truth. Sit down. I'll tell you what you want to know. Well, what I know anyhow."

Lily pulled back a chair at the small white round table and sat down across from Susan as she poured them both some more coffee.

"It was in the fall and we'd had a bad drought that year. Worst any of us had ever seen. Late in the afternoon, just a little while before quittin' time, I got the call at work from my sister Ellen saying the whole valley was on fire. We hadn't had any rain that year hardly and everything was so dry. It spread before anyone realized what was happening." She shook her head. "I mean, we don't have big fires around here that often."

Susan looked out the window as she talked, as if she was talking through another place in time. "Ellen said the fire was spreading too quick and was headed toward town, that we needed to get out of there as soon as possible. I tried to call my husband Sam, who was the mayor at the time, but he didn't answer. We both worked in town and most days we rode together to work, but that day we didn't. I drove down to his office by what was the courthouse back then, and they said that he'd gone home early but didn't know why." She smiled wistfully. "He was always slipping out somewhere, you know, so I didn't panic at first."

Susan shook her head and continued. "Come to find out, the fire had started at the Shelton Farm. What you saw is Carter's old home place where it burned." Tears began to form in Susan's eyes and she pushed them back.

"They found Sam and Carter's mother in the ashes of the barn. Everyone guessed he'd gone over to the Shelton place when the fire first started." She took a deep breath and shook her head "I don't know why he was there...Nobody will ever know for sure. I just know he's gone."

Lily reached over and gently touched her hand. "Oh God, Susan... I'm so sorry. I had no idea."

Susan shook her head, "It gets worse. Carter's father was helping with the fire in town. A building collapsed on him and three other firefighters. Carter lost every bit of family he had that day. Fourteen years old and suddenly he had a farm to run by himself."

"I guess he was in school when the fire started?"

"No, school had already let out, but he didn't come straight home that day. Good thing he didn't or they would have found his body right beside his mother's."

"No wonder he doesn't want to talk about it."

"He didn't talk about anything for about five years after that. One of the girls I worked with took us both in for a little while, until I could get my place fixed. Miraculously enough, the fire didn't do a whole lot of damage to the house. We lost a lot of cattle and one of the dairy barns – that's when I got out of the dairy business. Fortunately, our insurance covered it, but Carter wasn't so lucky. His mother didn't work, and his dad put very little back. There was barely enough to bury them both, let alone rebuild a house and barns."

"What did he do?"

"Well, the poor kid didn't have any family, and no options. All he had was the land, and that was it. I never had any kids and I needed help with the cattle around here. He wanted to quit school and go to work for me, but I wouldn't let him because I knew where it would lead eventually. So, we made a deal. If he would stay in school, he could work for me after school and on weekends, and

I'd make sure he had enough to pay the taxes on his land and have a little extra to put back every week to rebuild and whatever else he needed."

"I take it he graduated?" Lily asked.

"Oh yes, he graduated. With flying colors. His dad was a part time blacksmith and Carter picked up a little of it. That's when he headed off for ten weeks to a school in Oklahoma to learn how to shoe horses officially. He aced that too. He's been farming and shoeing horses ever since."

"He told me he wasn't certified!"

Susan laughed. "That's because he can't stand most certified farriers. Says they can't think outside of what they learned in school."

"He sure is cocky about his shoeing."

"Yes, he is. He's been doing it long enough. He's known for fixing everyone else's messes." She sighed, "Including some of the female species."

"Oh really?"

Susan nodded and took a sip of coffee. "He's had a go with several of the women I've rented to, if you know what I mean."

"Oh, I can just imagine..." Lily felt a twinge of jealousy at the thought of some other faceless woman in his arms.

"Shame such a good looking, hardworking man like him is still single at his age. He won't ever marry, I'm sure of it."

"Why not?" Lily asked a little too eagerly.

"I think losing his momma hurt him too bad. He's afraid to truly care about someone again. Grief will do that to a person, ya know?" She smiled wistfully and then asked, "What about you? What brought you here? What are you searching for?"

Damn, there was that question again. What was she searching for?

Lily pulled her defenses back up and answered, "Just a story Susan, just a story."

"Well, you keep telling yourself that, but I know better." Susan looked at her watch and stood up. "I've enjoyed the coffee and would to love to chat all day, but my cows aren't going to feed themselves."

Lily stood up and put her cup in the kitchen sink.

"Thanks for the coffee and the chat. I really appreciate it."

"Any time you want to talk about anything, just come on down. I'm here by myself most of the time, unless Carter drops by to check on me."

"I might just take you up on that," Lily told her as she opened the screen door and stepped out onto the porch.

"Wish you would."

Lily trotted down the steps into the damp morning mist. Even though it was close to nine thirty, the morning sun hadn't burned off the fog that hung below the pine trees nearby. It was a stark contrast to the dry, dusty heat in Susan's story.

As she walked back down the damp gravel drive, she suddenly remembered she'd forgotten to bring the key that she'd found in the ruins of the fire. Poor Carter. Now that she knew the story behind the fire, she knew she couldn't ask him about it. Of course, after last night's fiasco, she wasn't so sure she would see Carter again anyhow.

Chapter Seven

The talk with Susan lit a fire to Lily's muse. She was full of ideas and the beginning of a romance story was taking shape. A story of a small town hero with a disastrous past that falls in love with the town's floozy. It hit a little close to home, but Lily was inspired.

Writing a book was hard work, and normally, she would spend at least a full week ironing out characters and developing an outline for a plot. For the first time in her life, she sat down and started writing the first chapter without any of the usual formalities.

The words flowed effortlessly. Fueled by coffee in the morning, and wine in the evenings, she wrote with a furor she hadn't felt in years. It felt good to write, to feel the passion of creating a story that she was quickly getting lost in.

Four nights later, with wine glass in hand, she took a final look at the first three chapters she'd written. She felt good about it, perhaps better than any other romance she'd ever written before.

Taking a sip of the sweet red, she let the cool liquid slide over her tongue as she composed her email to Nate. A few seconds later, she took a deep breath and another sip of wine and hit Send.

Everything she had was riding on this story. She had no other choice. It had to be good. Although she'd been melodramatic before imagining flipping burgers at the local food joint, the truth was that might be exactly where she would end up if this story didn't pan out.

A few minutes later, her phone rang. She glanced at the time and winced. Nate was never up this late. Ever. She held her breath as she picked up the phone.

"What the hell have you been up to?"

Nate never cussed. This wasn't a good sign.

She swallowed hard and then answered, "Writing." She silently pushed a tear back that had made its way down her cheek and then added, "Maybe I just need to quit." The outward admission broke open the dam of tears she'd been holding back for weeks and she bawled uncontrollably.

"Quit? Oh no, you're not quitting!"

"Why not?" she sobbed. "There's no sense in me beating my head against the wall trying to do something that I just can't do anymore!" She dropped down on to the tattered sofa. "I suck as a writer!"

"No, you don't, Lily," he told her gently.

"I do! Get it over with and just tell me you hate it! I know that's why you're calling at two in the morning."

"No, it's not."

"Wait. What did you just say?"

"I'm not calling to tell you I hate it."

"Then why are you calling me when you should be in bed?" *With Jan*, she added to herself.

"I'm calling because I'm really excited. It's the best you've written in years, Lily. I don't know what you're doing...well, I might not want to know what you're doing... but keep it up. It's working."

Lily was about to let out a jump and squeal when she heard a vehicle pull up.

"Hang...hang... on," she whispered into the phone as she sat it down and peeked around the blinds of the front window.

Although it was dark, she could tell by the sound the vehicle was a pickup. Who would be coming to see her at this time of night?

"Lily! Lily! Are you alright?"

Nate's panicked voice coming from the phone on the couch suddenly reminded her that he was still on the phone. He was freaked out, but then, so was she with some stranger just outside.

"Hey…someone just pulled up in my driveway."

"Call the cops!"

"I'm on the phone with you. How can I call the cops?"

"Hang up, silly. Make sure your door is locked."

"But what if it's Susan and she needs help?"

"What if it's some redneck come to steal and rape…oh wait, never mind."

"Damnit Nate!"

"I'm joking. Is your door locked? Do you have a gun or something to hit them with?"

"No, I don't own a gun and yes, I have a…" She looked around for something she could swing if she had to. "I have a boot."

"A boot?"

"Well… or a meat tenderizer thingie."

"You're screwed. You got a kitchen knife?"

"Ah yes! One large one. I'll get that."

"Okay. Get that and then call the police."

"But what if it is just Susan?"

"Then you'll have called for nothing. Better safe than sorry. Now call!" He hung up.

She gripped her phone as she looked at it. What should she do? Lily didn't want to call the police over something stupid, unless maybe they sent a good looking officer. That might be a different story. Good Lord, had she been relegated to the old women that pushed their call buttons to conjure hot policemen? Ugh…. But she didn't want to end up dead either!

Her heart nearly jumped out of her chest when she heard the thud on the front door.

"Lily? Liiiiiiiily? I knnnooooowww you're in there! I seeee the lights on."

It was Carter. What was he doing here? She scrambled off the edge of the couch and jerked open the door.

Even though he was braced against the front of the house, he was weaving. His dirty gray cowboy hat was barely perched on the back of his head.

"Are you drunk?"

"I'm not quite sure." He jerked his head to the side and vomited violently, sending bodily liquids splattering all over the concrete porch and the front of the house. He wiped his mouth and then turned to her with a weak grin. "I might be."

"Oh my God, Carter." Just what she needed. A porch full of puke and a drunk cowboy at two A.M. - hadn't she out grown this? Oh well, the puke would have to wait until daylight. The cowboy, well that might be another story.

"What the hell are you doing here?" she asked as she grabbed his arm and helped him inside, and then grabbed the nearest trashcan because she was pretty sure there would be more puke.

"I don't know…" he said as he collapsed on her couch, sending his cowboy hat tumbling to the floor.

She picked up the hat and sat it on the nearby kitchen counter top. When she turned around, she noticed his tousled hair and fought the urge to smooth it.

"You can't even stand up and yet you drove. Do you know how dangerous that is?"

"Don't worry, I didn't drive on the road. I drove over the hill through the pasture." He gave her a silly smirk. "I have four-wheel drive, remember? I don't need a GP…a GP… whatever it is."

"GPS. I hope you didn't hit any cows."

"I don't think I did."

Her phone rang. She knew she better answer it before Nate called in the national guard for his revived best-selling author.

"Well, are you okay? You didn't call me back!"

"Yes, I'm fine. I..."

"Is that your boyfriend?" Carter sneered loudly.

She gave him an evil look and turned her attention back to Nate.

"Who was that? Are you okay?" he asked.

"It's just Carter. He's drunk."

"Carter?" he asked.

"Yeah," she told him as she walked into the bedroom and shut the door behind her.

"Who's Carter? That's kind of quick, Lily. It's been what, three months since the divorce?"

"Four or five, but who's counting? We're not seeing each other. He's just shod my horse, that's all."

"And that's why he's showing up on your doorstep so late? Look, I'll let you go. Send me the synopsis in a few days."

"Nate, what's wrong? You call me all excited wanting to talk about the book when you should have been asleep, and now all of a sudden you're different."

"Nothing's wrong. Just send me the synopsis." He hung up.

What the heck? It was as if he had flipped a switch. One moment he was joking and carrying on - the next he was all business, even a little cynical.

Maybe he'd had a fight with Jan. Although he'd never said a whole lot about their relationship and it seemed that they got along well, the few things he had said, and her intuition told her they fought a lot more than he let on. Oh well, Nate's mood could wait. She had to worry about what she was going to do with the very good looking, but very drunk cowboy on her living room couch.

As soon as she opened the door, she knew what she was going to do. He was kicked back and sound asleep, his long legs protruding over the end of the couch. She tugged his muddy boots off and set them by the door.

She sat down on the edge of the coffee table and looked at the tall handsome cowboy passed out on her couch. She reached out, stroked the side of his cheek. Although his eyes never opened, he suddenly grabbed her wrist and pulled her down to him, mumbling.

She put her hand out to catch herself and immediately felt the lean muscles of his chest and stomach. Before she realized it, she ran her hand over the length of his ribs, delighting in the feel of his firm muscles, and eliciting a faint groan from his lips. With the groan, however, came the putrid smell of vomit that jerked Lily back to her senses. She wrenched herself away from his grip and stood up.

With his dark messy hair, he looked innocent, almost a little younger, while he slept. Then again, that might be because his mouth was shut for the time being.

Knowing now what she did about his past, she wondered what he must have been like back then. How much had he changed over the years from the fourteen-year-old boy whose life suddenly changed in a disaster? She couldn't look at him now in the same light. Instead of seeing him as the good looking but somewhat of an asshole farrier, a part of her saw him as the vulnerable young boy whose heart had been broken at such a tender age.

Feeling a twinge of sympathy, she grabbed the fleece blanket from the back of the couch and laid it over him. Maybe in the morning she'd have a chance to ask him about why he showed up on her doorstep.

She left the sleeping cowboy alone and quietly made her way to her own bed. She dug out a pair of loose pajamas she hadn't worn in years and put them on. The old

Lily would have taken full advantage of such a gorgeous, vulnerable man sleeping on her couch. Not this time.

***

The bright light streaming by the edge of the shades woke Lily up from a sound sleep. She grabbed her phone from the nearby stand and checked the time. It was a little after nine in the morning.

Suddenly she remembered last night. She listened. No sound. Was he still asleep? She jumped out of bed and padded barefoot across the cool concrete floor to the door.

Her heart fell when she saw the empty couch. "Oh well." What was it exactly that she'd wanted to happen? She really didn't know.

She went to the kitchen and spied a handwritten note by the coffee pot.

Sorry about last night. Made you coffee. Maybe that will make up for my being a jerk.

-Carter

PS: Had to leave early. Didn't want to risk the chance of getting mooned again.

The simple note brought a smile. Maybe he wasn't still mad at her after all.

Chapter Eight

Lily expected to hear from Carter, but he didn't call. After a couple of days, she decided to take matters into her own hands. There was just too much she wanted to know, and the only way she was going to find out was to spend some time with him.

Dinner had been a little dangerous as there was too much time to focus on each other. She needed another activity.

She thought for a moment. A ride would be good but she didn't want to just call and ask Carter out on one. Then again, she hadn't ridden Mercado in a couple of days and there were trails everywhere, including over to his house, supposedly.

A good trail ride would give her a chance to iron her out her synopsis a little more, work her horse, and maybe see Carter. She could follow his truck tracks from the other night. This time maybe she wouldn't see any scary cows that would get her thrown.

It was late in the afternoon when Lily saddled up her gelding. She followed the tire tracks that led from her house, taking her across the top of the ridge for a little over a mile before dropping into a sage covered valley. A while back, she had passed the ruins that she now knew was Carter's childhood home. She was sure Carter's new home would be somewhere close but that hadn't been the case. She followed the tracks a good bit further before they ended at a gate that led to a small, single story log home with a barn right behind it.

So, this was Carter's place. It was very fitting for a bachelor cowboy. In fact, now that she thought about it, she really couldn't see him anywhere else.

The covered porch ran the full length of the front of the square log home, and overlooked a small deep creek a few yards below. At one end was a dark wooden swing and a huge rocking chair, just past a large chimney made of oversized rocks. It looked like something straight out of a Colorado ski lodge.

Slipping quietly down off her horse, she then slid his bridle over the rope halter she'd left on. She undid the lead rope she had fixed to her horn and tied the gelding to a nearby tree.

She didn't see Carter's truck. She guessed he was gone shoeing horses. She didn't want to be too nosy, but the curiosity of what his house looked like was killing her. Besides, it wouldn't hurt anything to just sit in the rocking chair on the front porch. Isn't that what you did in Tennessee anyhow?

Calling out his name just in case he might be around, she eased up the porch steps. There was no answer. As she neared the large arched front door, she noticed that it was slightly ajar. Rocking chair quickly forgotten, she held her breath and pushed the door open.

She stepped into a world completely unexpected. Instead of the typical roughhewn logs and cabin décor, the inside had an ultra-modern feel with clean lines and a concrete floor. The kitchen was stainless steel with concrete counter tops and open floating shelves. This was definitely not a cowboy abode.

Along the back wall, she saw the opening to what she guessed could only be Carter's bedroom. Looking around, she tiptoed toward the back room.

She pushed the door back a little too hard, causing it to bang loudly against the wall. She winced at the loud sound, but then screamed and jumped as someone's arms locked around her from behind. She hoped to God this really was Carter's house!

Not knowing who it was, she suddenly panicked. Kicking and wiggling, she struggled to get free, but she couldn't move, not even an inch.

"Let me go!" she screamed.

"Not on your life," he whispered closely in her ear.

"Damn you, Carter Shelton! You scared the hell out of me!"

"Good. You're kind of exciting when you're scared."

"Glad you got your laugh. Now let me go."

Not releasing his grip on her, he pushed her with the full length of his hard body toward the bed. Although he'd only meant to just tease her, the move was quickly backfiring as the feel of the curve of her ample butt against him was exciting him a little too much.

"Now, why would I let a trespasser go?" he asked as he nuzzled her ear playfully, pulling her even closer.

Lily sucked in her breath and pushed back against his hard member as the waves of electric shock went through her. "I didn't think..." A little moan escaped her throat.

Carter smiled. He was in control - this time. "You didn't think what?"

Not releasing his grip, he laced his fingers into hers and nipped at the curve of the base of her neck, causing her to squirm even more against him. Her struggle excited him, and at the moment, he wanted nothing more than to throw her on the bed and plow himself deep into her. But where was the fun in that? Lily was a woman to be conquered, and he knew it.

He did get her to the bed, but only to lay her down. Letting go of her hands just long enough to pull her shirt up, he resumed lacing her fingers in his as he nipped and licked every little inch along her ribs and back. With every nip came the glorious sound of her soft whimpers, which drove him up the wall.

The heat of his body against hers, paired with the feel of his mouth on her skin was more than her mind could bear. She had known a lot of men in life, but this one was driving her mad and he hadn't even hit third base yet.

As good as this felt however, she had to get a grip somehow. Her body yearned for him just as badly as his yearned for her. The nice bulge in his jeans made that pretty clear. If this happened, especially at this point of their knowing each other – or rather not knowing each other that well – then what? Where would one act of passion leave them?

It might not be a one night stand, but it wasn't exactly a committed relationship either. She didn't want casual sex, especially when a set of batteries could take care of that without any hurt feelings or complications. She wanted more, but she just didn't know what more was.

With all these thoughts managing to find their way through waves of pure ecstasy, Lily suddenly withdrew her fingers from Carter's strong grip. Summoning all her inner strength in one deep breath, she rolled over onto her back and looked up at Carter who was braced above her.

She traced the edge of his rough stubbled jaw. Damn, he was handsome.

"I like you, a lot. I want you, a lot," she told him as she laced her leg around his.

"I have something, if that's what you're worried about," he answered with a devilish grin on his face.

She bit her lip and shook her head. "Nope, that's not what I'm worried about, Carter."

"Now's not the time to be worrying," he told her, his voice husky and low as he nuzzled her ear.

"I know you don't think so, but I..."

Something in her voice made Carter roll on to his side, making sure, of course, her leg stayed entwined with his.

"I want you too, Lily," he said and looked down. "I think that's pretty obvious."

He pulled her closer to him and sighed as he looked into those fiery green eyes. She was more woman than he'd ever known, and more worldly too. Not that he was innocent, by any means.

Early on, he would have bet money he would have her bedded in less than a month, especially finding out how many times she'd been married. Before, that would have been just fine and eventually they would have gone their separate ways, each of them satisfied. Him the cowboy that couldn't be tamed, and her the woman that needed to move on. This time it was different.

"Look Carter, I didn't come here to get in this position."

"Well, what position did you want to get in?" His grin was a little too infectious.

"You smartass." She couldn't help but laugh.

Although her small moans of ecstasy excited him, her laughter filled a placed in him that hadn't been filled in a long, long time.

She shook her head and then told him, "Look, I know you're enjoying this, probably a little too much. I'm sure you feel like you're the cock of walk teasing me to the point of complete surrender, and I'll admit, I'm enjoying it myself."

"Yeah, I can tell." he smirked.

"But you know what? As much as I'm enjoying this, I don't want to be your entertainment, Carter."

The words made their mark into his heart, and they stung. He pulled himself loose and stood up, unable to say anything.

Lily bit her lip to keep her composure and then told him, "Look, I don't deny the fact that there's some fireworks going on, pretty hot fireworks, in fact. The problem is, I can't just leave it at that. I don't want to get hurt, and that's exactly what's going to happen."

He let out the breath he'd been holding and asked, "What makes you think I'd hurt you?" He regretted asking the question the second the words left his lips.

"Oh, c'mon Carter! Call a spade a spade. You're a player. I'm not some young girl that you can wrap around your finger. I know what your game is, and you're playing it with me already. You're good looking and charming, and you know it. The only reason you flirt is to get a reaction. It's entertainment for you, and a way to get what you want. I know that. It's not a new game to me. I may be lonely, but I'll be damned if I'm going to be the way you stroke your ego. I don't have time, nor any heart left for that."

The weight of her words cut him deep. She was absolutely right, he couldn't argue. She'd nailed him perfectly. Before, it wouldn't have made much difference. He'd been called a son of a bitch on more than one occasion by a woman that had fallen for him, but this time it hurt that Lily didn't think more highly of him than just a womanizer. He wasn't exactly sure why it made a difference.

Maybe it was because he'd gotten a glimpse of what lay behind that hard exterior of hers. She was tough, but there was a genuine sadness behind the toughness. He could only imagine the depth of hurt she'd experienced to keep it so well hidden, and that thought resonated with him deep down. He'd known a sadness too that he'd buried long ago.

He wasn't sure why her opinion even mattered, really. The only thing he was sure of was that her words stirred something deep down. He couldn't stand the feeling of knowing that she was angry at him. He grabbed her hand

and pulled her to her feet towards him, and then wrapped his arms around her, holding her close. He closed his eyes as he rested his chin on the top of her head and breathed in the scent of her soft curly hair. He didn't want to admit it, but he could easily get lost in being this close to her. He pulled back and kissed her on the forehead.

He took a deep breath and then let it out slowly. "Lily, you're right." He lifted her chin and looked into her misty green eyes that were full of hurt, and now confusion.

"I don't know what game you're playing, but you're damn straight I'm right." She pulled away from him as if the extra space would insulate her from what was going through her head at the moment.

She hated to admit it, but she liked him a lot – more than she should, and much more than she had intended. The casual flirting was quickly turning to something more than just a tease, and that wasn't good, especially considering his track record with Susan's previous tenants. He was just playing, and even though she knew that, she also knew she would get hurt in the end.

She despised the fact that she found herself thinking about him more and more, not to mention the spell he had over her every time he touched her. She didn't like being that out of control of her thoughts, or her emotions. It was a recipe for disaster, and she couldn't afford that emotionally, or financially.

"I'd better go." She turned toward the door.

"Don't go." He didn't want her to leave angry. In fact, he didn't want her to leave at all. The curious thing was that had it been any other woman, he wouldn't have cared.

Something in his tone of voice made her stop and turn around and search those dark eyes.

"Why? So you can have your fun?" she asked him.

The intensity of her inquiring eyes intimidated the hell out of him and excited him at the same time. He had to look away. "I know I don't have the best track record. I get that."

"And your point is?" She wasn't backing down.

"You're going to make me say it, aren't you?"

"Say what, Carter? What great mystery are you going to try now?"

She frustrated him beyond words, beyond his own understanding of what was going on within him. He only knew he wanted her badly, but it was different than he'd ever wanted any woman. It wasn't just purely physical, and he wasn't sure what to do with such an intense feeling.

Shaking his head, he cleared the space between them and pulled Lily fully against him as he tangled his hands in her hair and covered her lips with his. Her warm tongue met his with a fierceness that excited him even more. God, he could get lost in this. How was it that one simple kiss could make him want to inhale every single part of her?

She arched her body hard against him as her fingers dug into his strong shoulders as if to find some kind of release. She let out a small moan from deep within as he took her lower lip between his and ran his tongue along the edge. It was slow but intense, and the most sensual kiss she'd ever felt, leaving her breathless.

He pulled his lips from hers, and gently nipped along her ear and then down her neck to the tender skin along the top of her shirt. He reveled at the sight of the goosebumps his efforts had caused.

"I thought you were leaving," he teased huskily as he planted another firm nip just above her breasts.

"Ummm… I should."

"I don't want you to," He cupped her face with his hands and kissed her lips again, taking his time and enjoying the feel of her against him.

"Why don't you want me to go? Be honest," she asked him as she searched for some clue on his face.

He let out a sigh. but put his arms around her. "Because I enjoy spending time with you. Yes, I'm attracted to you and I like the reaction I get, but it's more than that."

"Carter, I don't want to fall for you and you're making it hard on me."

"So, what do we do?" he asked.

"I don't know, short of slowing things way down, but it's hard to put a fire out once it's started."

"We can try that. I mean, I can do it if you can," he teased.

"Oh, you've got a deal!" She teasingly punched his arm.

"What were you doing out here anyhow snooping around?" he asked, gently smoothing her tousled hair back from her face.

"I came here to see if you wanted to go trail riding."

"You didn't come here to sneak up and seduce me unexpectedly?" he asked as he playfully planted another kiss on her chest that sent shivers down her spine.

"No!" she giggled.

"So, trail riding was it, hmmm?"

"Yes! So, do you want to go or not?"

"I'd rather do something else, but for the sake of your sanity, we'll trail ride. I've got a horse out back that could use some miles."

"My sanity? Go get your damn horse!"

He gave her a mischievous smile and grabbed her hand, tugging her with him towards the front door. "I know you want to stay in my bedroom all day, but if we're going to go ride, you'll have to come outside."

"Carter Shelton, you're horrible!"

He looked back and winked at her and then replied, "That's not what I've been told."

Lily shook her head. He was such a smart ass, and there was no winning. But then, wasn't that the attraction?

She always did have a penchant for men that gave her a run for her money. The only problem was that sooner or later they wound up breaking her heart. Carter would be no different.

As they stepped off the porch, Carter nodded at Mercado who was standing with his eyes closed. "You can just bring him around to the barn."

Lily untied the sleepy gelding and led him to where Carter was saddling a sorrel gelding in front of the barn.

Contrary to the house, the barn was a traditional weathered red pole barn. With hay storage on one side, and four stalls on the other, it was a far cry from the high society barns she'd been around in west Texas and Arizona, but she liked it.

She watched Carter methodically saddle up the gelding that was dancing around.

"So, what's the story on this horse?" Lily asked him.

"He's a prospect I bought from the futurity sale. He's just three. He needs some miles on him. I don't get to ride him as much I'd like with everything that has to be done around here. A trail ride would do him good."

She looked the young horse over as Carter tightened the girth and grabbed a bridle off the wall. The gelding was well balanced and everything you'd look for in a barrel horse.

"You've got an eye for a good horse."

Carter beamed. "I've been told that a few times."

"Let me guess – by Susan's tenants?"

He laughed at the scowl on her face. "Maybe."

"See if I give you any more compliments."

"I bet you will," he told her as he pushed his hat back.

"I would not give you the satisfaction."

He winked and replied, "I'm sure if you're satisfied with me you would."

Lily's cheeks turned crimson, which was only made worse by Carter's full laughter.

"Cat got your tongue? Or maybe something else?" he asked her as he stuck his foot in the stirrup and stepped up on the red horse. "C'mon, get on your horse and we'll go out this gate."

Chapter Nine

Lily watched as Carter lined his horse up by the gate and side passed into it. The move was effortless; however, the young horse didn't want to stand still and kept dancing. Carter took a deep breath and relaxed in an attempt to get him to stand still.

"Sometimes he is a little high strung, of course he's fresh too."

"Sure you can handle him, with him being so fresh?" She regretted the words as soon as she said them.

He flashed his white smile and replied, "Darlin', I can handle anything that's a little fresh."

Lily rolled her eyes and waited calmly on her horse that was standing quietly underneath her. One thing she was pretty sure about, this wasn't going to be some relaxing trail ride. There were probably going to be a lot of moments like this.

Finally, Carter's horse relaxed, and he was able to open the gate.

Lily passed through and then told him, "I think I can close the gate."

"You mean that crazy barrel horse of yours will stand still long enough for that?"

Lily laughed at this comment and then proceeded to side pass into the gate until it was closed and latched.

"Not bad. Not bad at all." He told her as they followed a well-worn dirt path through the tall grass.

"So where does this go to?" she asked.

"It loops around and ends up over at your place. It's about a two-hour ride, or longer if you want it to be." He looked at her and grinned. "But now, I'd hate for you to take advantage of me while out on a trail ride."

Lily just shook her head and smiled. The thought of being in his arms again was appealing, but hell would freeze over before she'd initiate. A girl had to keep some sense of pride.

Much to Lily's surprise, the red horse settled into a ground-covering walk but didn't dance around as she had expected. Carter looked completely at ease sitting on top of the big gelding, and she guessed his calm manner had helped the horse relax. One thing was certain, he was a very good rider. For some strange reason, she hadn't expected that.

They rode in a comfortable silence for a while, side by side, following the rough red dirt trail as it meandered up and down the tall ridge, each lost in their own thoughts about the other. Sage replaying of the words Carter said that told her he wanted her to stay, and Carter struggling to figure out why this woman had such a hold on him.

Finally, Lily couldn't stand it anymore and had to say something to break the silence.

"Do you drive back here to check on things?" she asked. It seemed impossible to get even a four-wheel drive pickup down the road with its occasional deep ruts.

"I only take the four-wheeler out. No way the pickup truck can make it. I'll take the horses when I have time," and then he added, "You're always welcome to go with me." His smile was a boyish one, devoid of any mischief.

Lily noticed the change in his demeanor and wondered what had caused it. Whatever it was, as much as she enjoyed the playful banter between them, she really loved seeing this part of him.

"I would like that. How many acres do you have?"

"The farm is a little over three hundred acres. Decent for around here, but I know it's nothing like what you're used to out there in Texas."

"True, but you have so much more grass."

"Which is why we don't need as much land to run cows and horses."

"Yes, and it saves me some money on feeding Mercado, which I can use right now."

"So, how's the book coming along?"

The question caught Lily a little off guard, and she wasn't sure how she should handle it considering the topic was one that he didn't want to talk about.

"I sent the first three chapters and synopsis off to my editor a few days ago. I haven't heard back, but of course these things take time."

"If they accept it, what does that mean for you?"

"Well, I'm hoping they'll offer me an advance, which would certainly help my pocketbook. That would help open up opportunities again for speaking engagements at writer's conferences and that sort of thing. Plus, I might be able to land another movie deal, which would really be nice."

Carter stopped his horse in the middle of the trail. "Wait, you've written for movies? You never told me that!"

"Carter Shelton, there's a lot of things about me I haven't told you."

"I'm sure that's the truth! Can't say I'd blame you, they're probably not that flattering anyhow."

"You're incorrigible!"

"That's an awfully big word you're using."

Lily's face turned red in her failure to have a snappy comeback. She bit her lip and glared at him instead.

"Poor girl doesn't know whether she's coming or going," he chided as he moved his horse right up against hers. "But maybe this will make up for it," he said as he tipped her chin towards him and kissed her once again, this time a little gentler and slower.

For some reason, he couldn't bear to pull back after the kiss ended. He laced his fingers in her red curly hair at the base of her neck and looked into those deep hazel eyes speckled with small bits of gray. He was struck with the thought that they were the prettiest green eyes he'd ever seen.

"What?" Lily asked him softly.

He shook his head. "Nothing...not a thing."

As though the spell was gone, he sat up on his horse and legged him forward.

Lost in her thoughts, Lily let him get a little ahead. What was it he had been thinking? The man was slowly driving her insane.

"So, does this mean you're going back to Texas if they offer you a deal?"

His pointed question interrupted her thoughts. "I don't know. Maybe, maybe not. I haven't really decided."

"Well, everything is bigger and better in Texas. At least that's what I hear."

"Yes, that's what they say." She agreed with him, although Tennessee had been looking awfully fine here lately.

"You got family back there or something? Is that's what holding you there?" The thought of her going back to Texas irritated the hell out of him. Why was Texas so great anyhow?

"No. I don't have any family, at least not much to speak of. I just like barrel racing and Texas is familiar to me."

"You can barrel race here." The words slipped out a little too easily.

Lily legged the yellow horse up beside his and turned to look at him. "Does that mean you want me to stay here?" She noticed the flush of red as soon as she said the words.

He shook his head in frustration, "Nope, just saying you could."

What exactly was it that he was saying? Hell, he didn't know!

"What if I did stay here?" she asked him as she asked Mercado to move forward again.

"Well, if you sold your book, you could move out of Susan's."

It wasn't the answer she was looking for, but then she really wasn't sure what she was looking for. It was all a bit too much. Why was she suddenly feeling like she had to figure out her life at this very moment?

Carter trotted ahead of her up to the top of the ridge and stopped. "You can see the Smokies to the east and the Cumberland Plateau to the west. One of the best views in the area."

Lily caught up and came to a halt beside Carter. With the deep green mountains in the far distance on one side, and the violet tinted hills in the waning sun on the other side, the view was indeed breathtaking. This place was growing on her.

They continued down the ridge in relative silence until they came to where the woods opened up into a wide flat field.

Carter stopped his horse and grinned, "See you on the other side." The red horse bolted off into the field.

Lily scrambled to gather her reins on her palomino, now jumping sideways with excitement, almost unseating her. She dug her legs in, grabbed the over and under on the horn and gave her horse a firm swat on the haunches, sending him bolting forward out of his shenanigans.

She gripped her horn with her free hand and willed herself to give her horse its head as she urged him forward to catch up with the red horse ahead of her. Against every ounce of self-preservation, she was riding to win this sudden challenge from Carter. She knew if she chickened out, she'd never hear the end of it.

After the initial panic wore off, Lily settled into barrel racing mode and urged her horse to give her everything. Carter and the red horse were halfway across the field, but Lily was determined to catch them before they reached the other side. This was one race she couldn't lose.

Carter was enjoying the casual sprint across the field when he heard the palomino gaining ground from behind. He looked back to see Lily riding hell bent for leather and she was gaining on him. He kissed to his young horse, who gave him another gear.

The two riders raced neck and neck to the end of the field and when suddenly Carter remembered that there was a big ditch at the end of the field. He started slowing his horse, hoping that Lily would do the same, but she didn't.

"Slow down!" he yelled at her.

"No way, I'm not losing!" she yelled over her shoulder as she squeezed her horse up.

Carter reined his horse to a stop and winced as he watched the pair barreling towards the ditch hidden by the tall grass and sage.

Two strides out, Lily finally saw the ditch and let out a "WHOA!" as she tried to stop her horse. It was too late. The powerful gelding gathered himself and bounded across the ditch, catching a back foot on the other side and stumbling. Out of time with her horse, Lily wound up on the cantle and then was thrown forward.

"Son of...." Lily screeched as she grabbed for the horn and the reins and fought to find her stirrups.

Carter now laughed at the hot mess before him. She had grit if nothing else.

"You might need to get your heels down!" he teased her.

"Carter Shelton, you are an ass!" Lily replied as she brought the big gelding to a halt. "This was all your fault!"

"Oh, it was, huh?"

"Yes! You just had to take off across this field."

"I see…and you just had to follow because you couldn't control your horse, right?" His teasing was infectious.

Lily laughed and then shook her head. "Well, at any rate, I won."

"Only because I pulled up for the ditch that you almost didn't make it over. I thought I was going to have to call an ambulance. It was like watching a train wreck." Even though he didn't want to admit it, he did love giving her a hard time.

"I'm just glad I didn't hit dirt. That's the first time I've ever raced another horse, let alone across a field this big."

"What? You a barrel racer and you've never raced across a field? Are you sheltered or what?"

"Maybe a little," she conceded.

Carter guided his red gelding over the ditch to stand by the resting Mercado.

"You stay here long enough, I just might have to show you the finer points of living in east Tennessee."

Lily thoroughly studied the deep brown eyes and saw no hint of teasing. Against her better judgement she replied, "I would like that. A lot."

"We're only about ten minutes from your house going this way." Carter led the way down the narrowing trail through the sparse trees.

Lily now recognized the trail they were on. It was the one that she had followed down to the remains of the burnt house. If she played her cards right, maybe she could get some more information that might piece together where the key had come from and give her something for her book. As a writer, her gut told her the piece had to have a story behind it that was critical to the book she was writing. Now she just had to play dumb and see what she could find out from Carter.

As they rounded the bend in the trail and the valley opened up, Lily scanned the tree line until she saw the burnt wood. If they stayed on the trail, they would be passing right by it. Lily might get her chance.

"Gosh, it's so pretty here."

"Yep, it is." Carter sighed.

"Hey, what's that over there?" Lily asked, trying to sound naïve.

"Just some old burnt wood."

"Looks like a barn..." she pressed him.

"Yep."

She couldn't stand it. "Is that one of the barns that burned up in the fire all those years ago?"

"Yep."

"Well, this is your land. Was that your barn?"

Carter stopped his horse and shook his head. "Ok, Miss Reporter. If you have to know, yes that's my barn, and the house I grew up in. They both burned down in the fire. There, you satisfied?"

Lily noticed the clinched jaw. "I didn't mean to make you mad by asking questions."

"No, but you insist on bringing up things I'd rather forget...permanently."

"I'm just trying to understand, that's all."

"It burned, some folks died, the rest of us got on with our lives. There's not a lot to understand."

"There is if me merely asking what happened is making you this upset."

"Look, I moved on a long time ago. Hell, the whole town has. Why do you want to dig up the past to something that doesn't belong to you?"

His words made their mark. "Point taken. Don't worry, I won't ask about it again. In fact, I know my way back from here. I'm sure your horse is tired, and you've got a long way to ride back. I'll see you later." She trotted off, not giving him the chance to answer.

Carter watched as she disappeared over the hill. Damnit, why did she have to go digging up the past? A past he didn't want any part of and had fought every single day to forget. Leave it to a writer to go digging up bones.

Chapter Ten

Lily took a sip of strong coffee and read through the paragraphs she'd just typed out on her computer. It had been a full week since she'd heard from Carter and writing non-stop in the final push to get the first rough draft on paper had been a welcome distraction. Fortunately, the hard work was paying off. Not only was she almost finished, but focusing on the story had kept her from crawling back to the log cabin over the hill and making a fool of herself.

As she read the words, she smiled. This might just be the book to get her back on the map. The story was honestly better than anything else she'd written so far. Although Nate had not heard back on the sample chapters and synopsis, he was certain that the editor at Millington would want to see the rest of the book before they made a final decision on this new project after canning the last one. At least this time Lily knew she would have something good to send them.

She was making a few small adjustments to the manuscript when the phone rang.

"Hello gorgeous!"

"Wow Nate, you're in rare form. Gorgeous? Really?"

"Well, I have to have some way to keep my star writer."

"Says the man who told me to snap out of it a couple months back. What's up?"

"Well, I just heard from the editor. Just like I thought, she absolutely loves the synopsis and the sample, but she wants to see the rest of the manuscript before she makes it official. She said it would be perfect for their movie line once it runs as a book. When can you have the rest ready?"

"Can I have another week, or do you think that's too long? I'm working on the last chapter now and I've already done some earlier edits, but it could use a new set of eyes."

"I think I can put her off for another week but no longer than that. Send me what you have and I'll clean it up – don't get used to this," he chided.

She laughed. "Thanks Nate – don't worry, I won't. I'll send you what I have in a few minutes, and I should be done with this last chapter by this evening or tomorrow morning at the latest."

"Lily?"

"Yes?"

There was a long pause. "Once we get this deal, what are you going to do?"

"I honestly don't know. I haven't really thought about it."

"What about…what's his name?"

"Carter? Oh, I don't know…"

"Have you slept with him?" Nate grimaced.

"That's awfully personal!"

"I know, I know. I just don't want to see you…get hurt. That's all."

"Nate, when have you ever been so invested in my personal life? This isn't like you. What's up?"

"Nothing…. Nothing at all… I just… Look, get the manuscript to me as soon as you can, and we'll make this happen. You'll be on the New York Times list again before you know it. Talk to you later."

Lily hit the call end button and sat her phone down on the small desk. Although Nate had great news, something was off. He'd joked here and there about her love life in the past, but out of respect for his wife Jan he'd never been one to ask such personal questions. It was a business relationship where they knew a little about each other but that was it. The fact that he'd came right out and asked her point blank whether or not she'd slept with Carter didn't sit well, but maybe that would be the end of it once she sent the final chapter. She could hope so.

After a day of non-stop writing, she was ready for a break by late afternoon. She glanced at the time. Mercado would be ready for his evening feeding and turnout. Hearing the sound of soft rain on the tin roof, she grabbed a light jacket from the back of the kitchen chair and tugged it on.

Feeling the movement of something heavy in the pocket, she felt inside. She pulled it out and ran her fingers over the key.

"I don't guess I'll ever know where you came from or what your story is, but if nothing else you launched one of the best stories I've ever written," she told the faded metal as she laid it down on the edge of the kitchen counter.

Lily found Mercado waiting by his feed bucket. She dumped the handful of pellets in the bucket and then opened the panel gate and started cleaning the stall. She was just about done when she heard a diesel truck pull up at the front of the house.

"Lily?"

"Back here at the shed, Susan!" she called out. She waited until Susan was at the gate and asked, "What brings you down here in this drizzle?"

The older woman replied, "Just checking in. It's been a while." She made her way through the maze of trails in the tall grass. "I'm going to have to send Carter over here to bush hog for you." She shook her head. "Thought he would have done that by now."

"I didn't realize that was his responsibility…"

"I still pay him a little to keep some things up for me. Normally, I don't have to tell him, he just does it but here lately I don't know what's gotten into him…What's going on between you two, Lily?"

"I…uhhh… Susan…"

"I've known Carter his whole entire life, Lily. I know when something's bothering him. You two sleep together?"

"No!" Lily squealed a little too eagerly. "Oh God no… well, it's come close a few times, but no… I'm not going down that road again."

"Well, I can understand that…what do you mean again?" Susan asked.

Why did she always have to end up in a situation where she had to just tell everything? There wasn't any way out of this. "Why don't we go in the house and have a cup of coffee."

Lily turned Mercado out into the big field and made small talk with Susan about the soft rain and fog on their way back to the house.

"Please excuse the mess, I've been working on my book. Haven't stopped do anything else." She cleared the table and chairs so Susan could sit down.

"You know, every gal that's ever rented this place wasn't a saint. Whatever it is that you have to tell me won't surprise me much."

Lily decided to jump in with both feet. "Well, I just went through my fifth divorce."

"Good Lord!" Susan couldn't keep the words from slipping out. "I mean… we don't see that often around here."

Lily was reminded once again why she really didn't fit in to a small town. "I'm sure you don't." She busied herself with making coffee as she continued. "I've just always had a penchant for bad boys, I guess. Always fall too easy, too quick."

Susan's voice softened. "It's because you're looking for something."

Lily tilted her head to the side. "I guess you could say that...probably one of the reasons I'm a romance writer. I can't find the perfect relationship, but I can live it out on paper."

The older lady shook her head, "Nope, perfect doesn't exist. Perfect people don't exist. But you know what? There is true love. Might not always be pretty, but if it's honest and it's true it's worth it."

"You really believe that? Why haven't you re-married after all these years?"

"Oh Lily, I had my heart broken deeper than most folks will ever be able to understand. Besides, I'm okay with being alone as long as I can get somebody to do the stuff I physically can't."

"You might be onto something. That's what I meant earlier. I don't need complications. I need to get my career turned around." Suddenly she spied the key on the counter. She picked it up and handed it to Susan.

"What do you make of this?"

The color drained from Susan's face. "Where did you find this?"

"In the ruins of Carter's home and barn where he grew up. Why? You know who this belongs to."

She sighed. She recognized it immediately and felt the pain that went with it. "Yes, I do. It was a gift to Carter's mother."

"Why was it left there? You would think Carter would have wanted something personal of his mother's, especially since everything else was completely burned."

"Not all of us handle grief the same way, Lily. Carter was just a young kid that wanted to leave it all behind and forget about it. That's why he never tried to rebuild down there. I think he took it a lot harder than most folks realized…and I think he's having to deal with it now that you're asking questions."

"He said something to you…"

"He mentioned it."

"Well, what else has he said?"

"More than he realized. I think you're getting under his skin more than he expected. More than any of us expected, actually."

"I didn't mean for any of this to happen."

"I know you didn't but do yourself and Carter a favor. If you don't plan on staying around after you get this book written, don't pull him in. He may come across as the egotistical womanizing cowboy, and for a lot of women he has been, although he's always truthful from the very start. Underneath it all he's been searching for something too and whether he realizes it or not, he thinks he's found a little bit of it in you."

"Oh Susan, I don't know about that…". She didn't like what she was hearing.

"It's true. He's falling for you. I've never seen him so excited – or so moody - about a woman as I've seen him since you came along. Yes, he can be an ass, but he's got a good heart and he's been through enough."

Lily didn't say a word as she poured them both some coffee. Her mind was racing with the revelation that Carter might be falling for her.

Sensing she'd overwhelmed the fiery redhead, Susan changed the subject. "What about that book? Any chance I might be able to get a peek? I love a good romance. You know, I just finished your latest one."

"Oh really? How did you like it? Have you seen the movie?"

"Yes, I did! I actually saw the movie first and liked it, but after reading the book, I see the movie didn't really do the book justice. Such a great story. I loved how you brought them together."

"Yep, that was a story that came from real life. Husband number two."

Susan laughed. "I guess if nothing else you've lived a lot of writing material."

"You could say that."

Susan glanced at her watch. "It's getting about time for me to go feed cows. Give some thought to what I said." She got up and put her coffee cup in the sink and then added, "You know, sometimes you find what you're looking for in places you don't expect."

Lily smiled wistfully. "Sometimes."

Susan made her way to the door. "Holler if you need anything. I'll have Carter get on the bush hogging later this week."

"Thanks Susan… for everything."

"Any time."

Lily sat down on the faded metal chair on the front porch and watched as Susan disappeared over the hill in the fading light. This day sure turned out a lot different than she had planned. Suddenly she remembered Nate was waiting on her to finish the last chapter.

With the email to Nate finally sent, Lily settled in to finishing the last chapter on her book. She easily got lost in typing out the happy ever after ending. It was as if she were writing herself out of all her failures, not only her last failed story and her failed marriages, but the fact that she was utterly alone.

She worked with a fury late into the wee hours of the morning, completely focused on editing every line. Eventually, her eyes grew heavy and she fell sound asleep with her computer in her lap.

At dawn the next morning, Carter drove the Massey Ferguson tractor towing a bush hog into the driveway and cut the engine. He knew at this early hour Lily was most likely still asleep but considering her reaction the first time he came to shoe Mercado, he figured it was best to knock on the door and let her know he was there to mow the pasture.

He slipped off the tractor and walked up to the front door and knocked. There was no answer, so he knocked louder. Still no answer. He turned the door knob. It was open. He slipped inside and saw Lily still sound asleep on the couch.

For just a moment he admired the sleeping redhead with her tousled hair around her shoulders. She looked so peaceful and he couldn't help but think he possibly could get used to seeing that on a regular basis. Without thinking, he reached down and brushed the wayward strands back from her face. She stirred and opened those vibrant green eyes. She gave him a sleepy smile that melted his heart.

"Hey sleepyhead," he said softly.

Lily sighed and sat up. "What time is it?"

"A little after seven."

"Ugh…what are you doing here so early? And how did you get in?"

"I'm here to bush hog your pasture. Trying to beat the heat. Oh, and the door was open."

"And you just walked right on in."

He chuckled. "Well, I didn't want to get mooned and accused of trying to steal a horse again."

"You do have a point." Suddenly she remembered that Mercado was due to be shod again. "You didn't happen to bring your shoeing tools, did you?"

"No, but I can come back and shoe him this afternoon after I get done mowing."

"That will work. I'll have a week and half before the barrel race."

"You're going?" he asked as he headed to the door. With her sleepy look, it just wasn't a good idea for him to stay any longer than he had to.

"Yep. I think it's time I go have a little fun. Are you going to run your sorrel? Is he ready?"

"I might. Not sure yet." He walked out the door without saying anything else.

Lily sat there mystified by his sudden exit. The man was so infuriating! One minute he was nice, and she wanted nothing more than to be in his arms. The next he was as cold as ice. Well, at least she could get her horse shod later today.

She busied herself with getting cleaned up and then making coffee before settling in with the edits on her book. She was lost in thought when her phone rang.

"Hey..." She knew it was Nate. No one else ever called.

"You have to send me the ending. I can't stand the suspense!"

"Wow, I don't think I've ever seen you this excited about one of my stories."

"It's a good tale Lil, one of the best you've ever written. I think it's because you've actually let down a few walls and written from your heart. Look, I've got to go. Send me the ending!" He hung up before Lily had a chance to reply.

She did a silent happy dance and then quickly saved her work and sent the revision to Nate. God, it felt good to have someone interested in her work again. Maybe she could do this after all!

Chapter Eleven

Lily stopped for a break when she heard Carter leave on the tractor. Three o'clock. He would still have time to get the shoeing in.

A little while later she heard the truck pull into the driveway. She darted out the back door and headed to the barn. She already had the halter on the gelding when Carter came around the corner of the house. He quickly turned and headed back to his truck.

Lily led her horse to the front yard where Carter had already unloaded his farrier tools.

"So, how did he do with this first set of shoes? He looked like he was moving ok the other day."

"Yeah, he felt good."

"I'll shoe him the same way then. He's still got a way to go from your last shoer, but he's better than he was."

"Susan said you were used to cleaning up messes."

"Yep, I am."

Lily didn't say a word as she thought about what she'd just said. Apparently, Carter had cleaned up a lot of messes, and not just the shoeing kind. She felt a tinge of jealousy as she thought of the previous tenants.

Carter commenced to pulling Mercado's shoes and making small talk. "They have a bunch of money added for the barrel race. I'm guessing first place will pay around a thousand or so."

"I doubt we'd make first, but it sure would be nice to take home at least enough to cover my entry fees and gas."

"Maybe you will." He gave her a quick smirk. "This shoeing will help."

"Yeah, if he's not sore."

"He won't be sore on account of me."

"So, you've never driven a bad nail or trimmed one too short?"

"I can't say that, but it's been a long, long time." He held up Mercado's foot and checked the wall.

"By the way, Susan told me you went to farrier school and you're certified. Why didn't you tell me that?"

Carter shrugged his shoulders. "Didn't think it was important."

"So, you lied?"

"Nope, I just didn't tell you." He pulled off the last shoe and started clipping away the excess wall.

Lily shook her head. There was no winning with this Eastern cowboy.

Carter worked in silence for a bit and then he spoke. "Tell me about all these exes of yours. What was the attraction?"

"Wha....what?"

He hit a nail into the hoof and then continued, "Yeah, I mean where they all bad or what?"

"No...I mean...I don't know!"

"There had to be some reason they didn't all work out."

"Well, let's see. Husband number one needed to grow up."

"How old were you?"

"Eighteen. Too young to be married, that's for sure. We both needed to grow up."

"And husband number two?"

"Rebound. It didn't last six months." She figured she'd just get it over with and satisfy this sudden curiosity, whatever it was. "I stayed single for a couple of years and wound up with number three. He turned out to be an alcoholic. I love my wine, so that was a toxic relationship."

"That's quite a history. What about number four?"

"I married with my brain and thought I was doing the right thing. We were married for seven years. I actually sold my first book the few years we were married."

Carter finished shaping a shoe and then asked, "What happened? Sounds like you were happy."

"I was at first. When I started to find success as a writer, then things changed. I think he felt threatened by the fact that I was successful in my own right."

"He wanted his little woman at home, pregnant and barefoot?"

"Pretty much, except I didn't want kids." Lily laughed.

The unexpected sudden image of Lily with a kid hanging off her hip danced through Carter's mind. "Why not?"

"Eighteen years with the same person raising a kid is a long time. That takes a lot of trust and I didn't want to do it on my own. It's best I never had any."

"Yeah.... what about your family? You never talk about them."

"Carter, what is it with all these questions and sudden interest?"

"Just curious, that's all."

"Susan must have had a talk with you."

He taunted her. "We talked."

"Oh really?"

"Yeah."

"And?"

"What about your family?"

"My mom died of an overdose when I was sixteen. I have a half brother and sister that I have no idea where they are. I never spent time with any aunts or cousins or anything. There, you satisfied?"

"Husband number five?"

"Hell. Absolute hell and it almost broke me in more ways than one."

"So now the truth comes out."

"I told you why I was here."

"Yeah, you said your book got cancelled and you were broke but it sounds like more than your pocket book got broke."

"You could say that."

"Well?"

"Fine. He was younger, rich, knew all the right people and was too good to refuse."

"Until you found him with your best friend."

"Yeah, until I found him with my best friend....and he took everything in the divorce."

He didn't know why but he felt for her. He felt her pain.

"You're a broken woman, aren't you?" he said as he drove in another nail.

Lily bit her lip and fought back the tide of tears. "How far is it to the barrel race?"

Carter shook his head and set the gelding's foot down. "An hour or so. It's easy to get to. Take I-75 to 40 west." He finished Mercado's hoof.

Lily shifted her feet and played with the end of the lead rope in the uncomfortable silence as he worked. Damnit, Carter had a way of seeing past the walls she put up.

"Trot him off when you go to take him back to the barn. I want to see how he's moving."

Lily turned Mercado around and trotted him in the direction of the barn.

Carter watched the horse's footfalls to make sure they were even, "He looks good!" His eyes drifted to Lily's round hips as she jogged alongside Mercado and added quietly as he smiled, "Yep, not bad at all."

Lily put Mercado in his stall and came back to find Carter packing his tools up.

"I've got some cold pop in the fridge if you want to come inside and cool off."

Carter shut the gate on his pickup and followed Lily into the house. As he stepped into the coolness, he grabbed Lily by wrist and pulled her against him. She gasped but he covered her mouth with his before she had a chance to say a word. He kissed her long and hard.

"I've been waiting all week to do that," he murmured in her ear as his hands pulled her hips against him.

Lily smiled slyly at him and then pulled away. "That's why you told me not to stick my nose where it doesn't belong and didn't call for a week?"

He shook his head in frustration, "Damnit Lily, I'm sorry."

She saw the key at the edge of the counter and grabbed it and held it up in front of him.

"Where…where did you get that?" Carter hissed.

Her heart raced as she answered him quietly, "In the burned ruins of your old place."

"And just what did you plan on doing with it?"

She took a deep breath and replied, "Ask you about it and give it back to you."

"Hell, I don't want that damn thing." He fought to keep her from seeing the tears stinging his eyes. "So, that's what this… this thing between us… was all about, huh?"

"What do you mean?"

"Don't play naïve with me, Lily. You knew exactly what you were doing. Anything to get the story for your next book. You're a writer, remember?" He spat the bitter words out.

"No Carter…that's not what this – whatever *this* is. I don't need a story that bad."

He smiled wistfully. "Oh, but you're a broke writer."

His words stung. "Thanks for reminding me. By the way, I'm curious. Just what is *this* between us Carter, since you mentioned it?"

He shook his head. "Nothing. Nothing at all."

She bit her lip and then nodded. "Well, okay then." She turned to the refrigerator and pulled out two drinks and handed one to Carter. "You can take this with you after I get your payment from the back room."

Lily held her tears until she closed the door behind her. She made futile attempts to push them back as she dug blindly through her purse to find enough cash to pay Carter. She laid the cash on the bed and went to the small bathroom to freshen up. She looked at her flushed face in the mirror and doused the red skin with some cold water. There was no way she could hide the fact that she'd cried. He had hurt her pride more than anything.

Damn him. Damn his cold heart. Although things hadn't got to the point of taking clothes off, she still felt like a cheap piece of ass. She should have known better than to get involved with another cowboy. Lesson learned. She was just glad that things hadn't gotten any further than a few heated moments.

She pulled herself together, grabbed the money off the bed and went out to pay Carter.

"Here's your money for shoeing Mercado." She met his eyes with determination.

Carter felt a twinge of guilt as he saw the hurt in Lily's eyes. He shook his head. "Don't worry about it. You don't owe me anything."

"I'm not taking your charity."

"It's not charity…"

"Take it, Carter. I'm not that bad off." She could use the money, but she'd be damn if she'd let him know that right now. Sometimes a girl had to have her pride.

"No, I shouldn't have said what I did."

"You said what you honestly thought."

"No...." Why did things have to be so hard with her?

"Damnit, just take the cash and go." She laid the cash on the counter and turned her head to keep Carter from seeing the tears that were starting but it was too late.

"Lily..." he said softly.

"You need to leave," she told him without looking at him.

The coldness in her voice hit him hard. In one swift moment seeing his mother's key had brought back the anger and hurt he'd buried deep – and he'd taken it all out on her. He shook his head and walked out the door.

Tears streamed down her face as she slammed the unopened drink across the room, almost knocking over the computer that was sitting on the coffee table. She waited until she heard the diesel truck pull out of the driveway and poured herself a large glass of wine. It was time to pull herself together. She had a book to finish.

With red wine fueling her muse, it was the wee hours of the morning when she finally typed out "THE END". Already a bit tipsy, she took another sip and scanned the last chapter. She smiled wistfully. Her own life might be a disaster, but the small town girl in her romance would live happily ever after with the man of her dreams.

She hit Send, and then shut the lid on her computer. She put her glass in the sink when her phone rang. She glanced at the time when she picked it up.

"How's my favorite writer?" It was Nate.

"It's 2 a.m. and you sound chipper. It's the middle of the night. You should be asleep...with your wife."

"Well, my wife isn't here, and I'd rather talk to you."

"What is going on, Nate? You're not acting like yourself."

"Just reading the best ending you've ever written."

"Where's Jan?"

"What difference does it make where Jan is? I'm talking to you."

Nate's evasiveness didn't sit well. "I take it you liked the ending?"

"Perfect. Absolutely perfect and unexpected."

"Let's hope the editor likes it as much as you do."

"Oh, she will. So…what are you doing? Why aren't you out on a date or…something?"

What was it with his sudden interest in her personal life? "I had a book to finish, remember?"

"Yeah, but I didn't think you'd be alone. It sounds like you're alone."

"Where is this going, Nate?"

"I'm just interested in how you're doing."

"Why?"

Nate sighed. "Because I care, that's all."

She didn't know how to take his response. Was it purely platonic, or was he hinting at something more? Then again, maybe her imagination was going off the deep end. She had been drinking, after all.

She decided it was safest to change the subject. "When are you going to send her the last chapter?"

"As soon as I get off the phone with you, I'll read through it and make changes as needed and then send it."

"Sounds good, Nate. Well, I need to get to bed."

"Okay…" There was an uncomfortable silence.

"Keep me posted. Good night, Nate." She didn't wait for him to answer and hung up.

As she settled into the covers, she thought about the strange conversation with Nate. What had he meant? Was she jumping to conclusions about his comment that he cared? Was he making a pass at her, or was it totally innocent?

She let her mind consider if Nate had been making a pass. Even though they had a partnership for a few years, she had never met him in person. She wasn't sure of his age, but she guessed he was almost forty. From the pictures she'd seen, he was a handsome man with salt and pepper hair and a fit physique. She knew from conversations in passing that he regularly worked out at the gym.

Nate understood her and accepted her. At least he seemed to. It would be a perfect match, a writer and an agent. A life with him wouldn't be too bad. As she drifted off to sleep, her thoughts were filled with Nate and possibilities.

Chapter Twelve

A week passed with no word from Carter. With the way their last discussion had ended, she figured other than the routine shoeing, she wouldn't be hearing from him. It was over – whatever "it" had been. She spent the week mourning over something that apparently never was and kept herself busy with the edits on her story.

She had talked with Nate several times throughout the week, but strangely enough he was back to his normal business self. It seemed both chances at romance were back to where they were when she came to Tennessee. She felt alone.

This morning was a little different however as she had something to look forward to. It was the day of the barrel race. She was filled with a combination of excitement and nervousness. It was the first time she would be going to a barrel race without knowing anyone that would be there. Well, Carter would be there. She wasn't sure what to expect, whether he'd act like he didn't see her or if he'd speak. She didn't like not knowing.

She fed Mercado early and then inventoried her tack in the trailer to make sure she had everything she needed for the barrel race. She then packed a cooler and loaded it into the trailer.

She picked out a comfortable pair of jeans and a sleeveless shirt from her closet and put them on. As she looked at herself in the mirror, she was pleased with how she looked. She hoped Carter would notice, and then she checked that thought. She needed to focus on racing, not a cowboy that wasn't hers.

A little while later she was loaded up and on the road to the arena. It felt good to be headed to a barrel race on an adventure.

As she pulled into the gravel parking lot, she scanned the sea of trailers and absently looked for Carter's rig. She saw the black stock trailer and red truck. He was there. Her heart quickened a bit and she told herself to calm down.

She found a grassy spot at the edge of the gravel to park her trailer. There was a small amount of shade and she was a good way from where Carter was. She backed her truck into the spot and cut the engine.

She took a big breath trying to calm her nerves. "Ok, let's do this."

She hopped out of the truck and went to open the back doors of the trailer so Mercado could get some air. It felt strange being at a race and not knowing anyone. She felt like a kid at a new school and kept her head down as she walked towards the arena.

As she was looking down, she didn't see the person who had just stepped around the end of a trailer and plowed right into them.

She gasped at the impact into the other person, "Oh God, I'm so..." As she looked up to see the person she'd just walked into, her heart dropped.

"Well, I see you made it." He wasn't smiling, but Lily could see the mischievousness just beneath the surface. She wouldn't give him the satisfaction of seeing her smile.

"Yes, I did. I'm sorry I almost ran into you."

"Well, as long as you don't run over me with that horse of yours, I'll be good."

She wasn't going to break. "I'm sure that won't happen."

Carter watched as she walked off. Her anger just brought out the beautiful fire in her. He had the urge to stop her in her tracks and pull her to him, but he'd be damned if he was going to swallow his pride and let her know he wanted her. She had a hold on him and he didn't like the feel of it.

A little while later, she had saddled up Mercado and rode to the warm-up pen before her exhibition. She lapped the pen at a walk, letting him see the sights and get acclimated. She had set up practice barrels in the field at the house, but it had been at least six months since his last race and Lily wasn't exactly sure what to expect. He was a seasoned barrel horse, but Lily knew he could be unpredictable every now and then, especially if he was fresh.

As she lapped the pen, she saw Carter talking to a blonde beside a trailer in the parking lot. Lily noticed the much younger woman was wearing a skimpy athletic top and was extremely toned. She also noticed Carter seemed at ease with her, listening intently to whatever it was she was saying and then laughing heartily.

Jealousy burned in the pit of Lily's stomach as she watched them chatting effortlessly. She legged Mercado a little too hard as she asked him to bump up to canter and he bucked slightly in protest, bringing her back to the task at hand – she had to get her horse warmed up before her practice run.

She tried her best to focus on Mercado, but the blonde had stepped up on a bay horse and was making her way toward the pen too, with Carter in tow on his sorrel.

Lily pretended to be working on trotting some circles when they both entered the pen. Hopefully they would go about their business and let her complete her warmup.

Carter and the blonde lapped the edge of the sandy pen at a walk, still happily chitchatting as they went. Carter never looked in Lily's direction that she could see out of her peripheral vision, but kept his eyes turned to the blonde.

Lily turned her head ever so slightly to try to hear the conversation but couldn't make out what they were talking about.

Finally, Lily decided Mercado had enough bending and canter and decided it was time to head back to the trailer. She glanced at her watch. Exhibitions would start in fifteen minutes, if they started on time.

Carter and the blonde were walking up the rail towards the gate when Lily walked through leaving the pen.

"I shoed that yeller horse right there," Lily heard Carter tell the blonde.

"Looks like you did a good job, Carter. He's a nice horse."

"He's alright."

"I've not seen her before. Is she from around here?"

"Nope, she's from Texas."

"What's she doing all the way back here?"

"Working on a story. She's a writer."

"Oh, that's nice. I don't read. Don't have any interest. So how do you think your red horse is going to do?"

Lily was tempted to say something. In fact she was burning to make a comment, but she thought it best to act like she didn't hear a thing. She knew if she said something to Carter, there would be nothing but drama. So, she bit her tongue and rode Mercado back to the trailer thinking about how Carter had described her just like any other stranger and the fact that she really wasn't surprised the young blonde didn't read.

The practice runs were starting shortly, and she was early on the list, but she didn't want to hang out by the holding pen waiting for her run. She knew she would just be setting herself up for a confrontation at some point with Carter. It was best to just hang here by herself and avoid the drama.

She busied herself with getting Mercado settled at the trailer and then went on the hunt for water. She saw a faucet at the end of one of the barns and headed in that direction. She didn't hear Carter riding up as she turned on the faucet and filled her bucket.

"I see you've gotten settled in." Lily jumped slightly at the sound of his voice. "I didn't mean to startle you."

"Just wasn't expecting it."

Carter nodded, unsure of what to say next. He wanted to apologize for how he'd acted the other night. He had missed her like crazy, more than he'd ever expected to and yet he'd told her she meant nothing. He knew his words had hurt her and he could still see the hurt in her eyes now, even though he knew she was trying to hide it.

He hopped off his horse and reached for the water bucket. "I'll carry this for you."

"I can carry it myself. I figure your little blonde probably needs her water carried."

Carter caught her by the shoulder as she turned to go and pulled her towards him. "Set the bucket down."

She shook her head and did as she was asked, still trying to remain calm. Her pulse was racing at just the mere touch of his hand. Why did he always have to have this effect on her? She closed her eyes and tilted her head as he gently brushed a stray hair back.

"Try as you may, you can't help but react to my touch, can you?" He brushed her lips with his. "If that was my blonde, why would I have just kissed you? Hmmm?" he murmured against her ear, teasing her and sending shivers up her spine.

He had a point, but at the same time Lily couldn't help but feel as though he was just toying with her.

Lily closed her eyes as she fought between giving in to the touch and love she so longed for and keeping her pride. "Carter, I don't know what game you're playing, but the only game I want to play right now has three cans. I need to think about running my horse. I need the money, remember?" She pulled away without looking at him, grabbed her full water bucket and walked to her truck.

Carter fought the tears that suddenly welled up as he let her go and watched her walk back to the trailer. Damnit, why couldn't he have just told her how he felt? Why did he always have to tease her like all the other women he'd known in his life? She was different. She was too smart for that and deserved more – a lot more – and yet he had been unable to give her that part of him that was real and didn't toy with her emotions. Was he really that damaged from everything that had happened in the fire? Damn that day. Damn his mother for doing what she'd done.

***

Lily offered Mercado some water as Carter's words swirled in her thoughts. She cared way too much for him to let him play with her feelings. Hell, she was thirty-five for God's sake. Playtime was well over! She needed to focus on making a good run and funnel her anger to making a great run.

Once the gelding had finished drinking, she sat the bucket down, put his bridle back on and tightened her cinch. "Time to go run boy," she told the big palomino gelding as she put her foot in the stirrup and stepped up. It felt good to be racing.

By the time she made it over to the arena, a few riders had already run their exhibitions. She knew she was early on the list, so she eased her way to the large holding pen at the entry gate in between runs.

She took a deep breath and smoothed Mercado's braids. "It's only a practice run to let us get our feet wet." she told herself as she glanced around at the countless strangers waiting on their run and watching from their horse's backs.

"Next set up after the drag are numbers 35 to 45. Zach McCurdy, Dana Sawyer, Lillie Starr, Margaret Caldwell..."

All the color drained from Lily's face. Did she really just sign up with her pen name instead of her anonymous real name? Oh God, she must have! It had gotten to be such a habit from all book signings she'd done over the years to sign her pseudonym she hadn't thought anything of it. Still, how could she be so stupid?

Her hands shook as she concentrated on walking her horse around in circles at the edge of the large holding pen. Keeping him moving was more for her nerves than for getting him ready to run. He knew the drill, but Lily was rusty and now she was deathly afraid someone would recognize her for who she was and see how terribly she rode!

She was drowning in her thoughts when the little blonde that Carter had been talking to earlier rode into the edge of her circle and stopped, "Hey!"

Not seeing her until the last minute, Lily jerked her horse to a stop. 'What?"

"Oh, I didn't mean to stop you. Sorry about that." the blonde said in the sweetest Southern syrupy tone. "I just wanted to ask.... Are you the same Lily Starr that wrote the movie Always and Forever? I just loved that movie! It was a woman named Lillie Starr that wrote it and Carter said you were a writer."

Lily took a deep breath and weighed her options as she asked Mercado to start walking again. If she was insufferable or untruthful she might lose a fan, but if she was honest and then made a fool of herself, it would be just as bad. She'd heard barrel racing in the south was stock full of drama and she didn't need that.

"I'm sorry, I need to concentrate on getting my gelding ready to run," she told the younger girl over her shoulder as she continued walking the circle. Fortunately, that did the trick, and the blonde had walked off to her friends at the other side of the pen.

"Crisis averted, Mercado." The horse's ears twitched back and forth as he listened.

The tractor driver finished dragging the arena and two runs later Lily heard her name. It was time to go. She took a deep breath, gathered her reins, pushed her heels down and eased the now alert gelding into the alleyway.

The gelding danced sideways down the alley, pushing against the reins. As they lined up to first barrel, Lily grabbed the horn and pushed the reins forward, letting the gelding go to do his job.

Mercado got a bit more of a jump on her than she'd expected. The jerk backward rattled Lily and she fought to catch up, losing focus as she was heading to first at a faster pace than what she was comfortable with.

Riding a little behind and not able to set him up for first, Lily tipped the first barrel coming out of the turn. By the time she approached second, she had managed to pull the run together a little better and kept the second barrel up.

Mercado had picked up some momentum coming off of second into third and Lily had to check him for the last turn. The move caused him to rate a little harder than Lily expected, sending her forward just a bit. She managed to stay seated around her turn, but it wasn't the pretty barrel she'd hoped for and she fought to catch up as the palomino gelding blasted off towards home.

Lily pulled on the reins, but Mercado didn't come to an abrupt stop until the end of the alley, sending her up slightly in her seat again as they stopped. Lily rode to the edge of the holding pen and stepped off, loosening her cinch with shaking hands.

"Well, at least that fiasco is over," she told Mercado as she pulled the reins over his head. "None of that was your fault, I'm just rusty from not running."

As she left the pen headed to the trailer, the blonde was suddenly at her side again. "You ARE her, aren't you? Carter said you were. I watched your run. Are you running in open?"

"Take a breath," Lily snapped, never letting up her stride.

"Oh my. I'm…I…I know I talk fast when I get excited and well…you're a celebrity and all."

Lily stopped and turned to the young girl and gathered all the niceness she could muster. "Look, I really appreciate the fact that you love my movie – thank you. But I really need to get to my trailer, okay?"

The blonde just nodded as she watched Lily walk off. As she turned to head back to the pen, Carter came walking up.

"I see you met Lily."

"Yeah, you could say that."

"What happened?"

"She didn't want to talk."

"Well, she hasn't had the best of days."

"Yeah, I saw her run."

Carter didn't say it, but that wasn't what he meant. He knew he'd hurt her more than she'd ever let on. The pressure of being under the microscope in the barrel pen certainly didn't help.

"Well, I have a run in a few. Make sure you watch so you can tell me what I need to work on."

"Will do." He told her as he headed to the far end of the bleachers to watch the runs.

He settled in on the end of the wooden bench and propped his feet up in front of him. His gaze drifted out to the end of the parking lot where he saw the familiar palomino gelding tied to the back of the trailer.

He shook his head and tried to concentrate on the practice runs in the pen, but he couldn't. He hadn't been able to think of anything else but her. He knew she tried not to show it, he could see the hurt in her eyes even today. He felt like such a jerk for hurting Lily's feelings.

He had pushed the hurt from the fire so far down inside he thought he'd never see it again, but Lily changed that. She had managed to catch him off guard more than once with talk about it and she just wouldn't let go. He hadn't meant to be so harsh, but it brought up something deep and dark within him that he couldn't deal with and now it was costing him any chance of a future he may have with her.

He was lost in his thoughts when the blonde rode up to the end of the bleachers. "You see my run, Carter?"

"Um… Yeah. Yeah I did." Although he'd watched her runs, his thoughts had been on Lily the whole entire time and could barely remember any details.

"Carter…what's bothering you? Is it that Lily woman? Something going on between you two?"

"Now, Savannah, you worry about your run and I'll worry about my love life."

"Oooooh. The cowboy nobody could catch has finally been caught."

Carter's face turned crimson. "I… I… Just go run your horse."

Savannah laughed and called "Good luck" over her shoulder as she rode off.

He'd been trying to hide how he felt just as much as Lily had, but it obviously wasn't working. His pride and deep wounds however were still strong enough to keep Lily at bay.

Chapter Thirteen

Lily was waiting on the competition to start and had just settled into her chair in the shade when her phone rang.

"Hi Nick"

"Well hello, gorgeous!" he said just a little too eagerly.

"What in the world has you in such a good mood? Sounds like you're in an airport. Are you traveling?"

"Just glad to speak with my favorite author, especially when I have good, no *great* news – and yes, I'm traveling to L.A."

"What great news? The editor already said she wanted the book."

"Yes, but I pitched the idea of a three-book series from this book – sorry I didn't tell you that – and she wants that as well. You better get to writing!"

Lily squealed and leapt to her feet, jarring Mercado from his restful sleep at the side of the trailer.

Nick smiled at the sound of Lily's excitement through the phone. "Wait… there's more."

"What? Tell me! I'm so excited I can't stand it!"

"Well, the editor put me in touch with a producer that works with them often on movie projects. That's who I'm going to meet. They're interested in making a movie out of the book. I told them you'd written the script for the last two movies and they're anxious to get started."

"Oh my goodness Nate, I can't believe it!" Lily squealed.

"I'll be meeting with the head guy here in a few hours. I may be conferencing you in by phone if needed. Are you going to be around?"

"Yeah. I mean I'm at a barrel race and I may have to run and then call if that's ok. It's only for fifteen seconds anyhow…well, if you're fast." She giggled.

"You know I don't understand any of that horse stuff Lily, but I get it. Look, I've got to get off of here and get through this airport. I'll keep you posted by text. If I have to call you, I'll try to let you know ahead of time, so you can get off your horse."

"Okay, sounds good."

"Oh, break a leg or whatever it is they say to you cowgirls."

Lily laughed. "Good luck will suffice."

"Good luck then."

"Nate… thank you. You mean more to me than you'll ever know. You've given me back my life."

"I don't know what to say, Lily, other than I feel the same way. We'll be talking soon. Real soon."

Lily squeezed her phone and then did a celebratory dance beside her trailer. Little did she know that Carter was watching from the bleachers across the parking lot. He figured she must have gotten good news about the book that she was working on – the one thing that was driving them apart.

He shook his head. He figured she would be leaving soon, headed back out west where she came from, and where she belonged. There was nothing to keep her here if she sold her book. He put his hat back on his head and went to look for something to keep him occupied and his mind off of Lily who would be leaving anyhow.

Lily's celebration was short lived in the quiet after the phone call as she realized there was no one else but Mercado to share the good news with. Suddenly the world felt big and lonely. She'd just gotten the best news of her career and no one cared except for Nick.

She glanced at her watch again as she was getting restless with the sudden feeling of loneliness and the nerves of racing. It was a full hour before the race would start and she was in the second drag and would be running early. Maybe a leisurely ride on Mercado around the facility grounds would calm her nerves and warm him up at the same time.

A few minutes later she was mounted up and making her way towards a grassy trail at the back of the parking lot. She had no idea where it went, but anywhere was fine as long as she could burn an hour and get her mind on something else.

The trail was narrow as it wound through a patch of white pine trees. Lily had to duck several times as she followed the path along the hill. She was ducking under a sticky pine limb when she saw a familiar bay horse just up ahead. "Oh geez…" she said under her breath.

She wanted to turn around but there wasn't enough room, and it was too late. The blonde had already looked back and noticed them. She kept forward, slowing Mercado's stride hoping that the other girl would go on up the trail. Instead, the blonde stopped.

"I see we've run into each other again. My name is Savannah."

Lily took a deep breath. She really wasn't in the mood to talk, but for whatever reason this girl kept showing up, and it was never wise for a writer to be rude, especially to a fan.

She forced a smile, 'Hi, Savannah. And yes, I'm Lillie Starr. Actually, my name is Lily Perkins. I didn't mean to sign up as Lillie Starr for my run, just habit and I wasn't paying attention. I really had rather remain anonymous, if you know what I mean."

Savannah nodded and then added, "Well, Carter Shelton sure knows who you are. No doubt about that."

Lily's pulse jumped slightly at the mention of his name. "Yeah, he shoes for me. Does a pretty good job."

"Oh, it's more than that." She laughed. "You've got him all tore up."

"All tore up? What does that mean?"

"It's plain as the nose on your face. He's got it bad for you. I've never seen him like this. He didn't pay any attention to my practice run, and normally he would be picking that thing apart."

"Well, I figure Carter has the choice of a lot of women much younger and prettier than me."

"Oh he has, many times."

Lily felt a twinge of jealousy in the pit of her stomach and wondered if the blonde up ahead was speaking from personal experience.

"This trail ends up by the indoor arena where they're having the race. They'll be starting in just a few more minutes. Most of the time, they start late but today they're right on time."

"That's good, I'm running in the second drag in open."

"I'm not running until the end. I usually come out here to kill some time. I get bored if I sit around for too long."

"I see."

"So, what brought you here to east Tennessee? I mean, there's nothing here."

Lily sighed, "Needed a new start," she replied honestly.

"I figured somebody like you would have it made, a big writer and all."

"I did, until this last husband took me for a ride and took everything."

"So you're broke."

Lily laughed. "Yeah, you could say that."

"What about your books? Don't you make a lot of money off of them?"

"I do better than most, but sales vary from month to month and you have to release a new book frequently to stay relevant."

"Didn't you have a new book you were working on?"

"I did, but it got canned by the publisher."

"So, it wasn't any good."

"That's what my manager said. I just needed a fresh start and to find myself again. It's hard to write well when your heart's not in it."

"You came here to get a story."

"Yeah, I did."

"Well, did you get one?"

"Yes, as a matter of fact I did."

"Is it going to be a movie? I don't really read but I love movies!"

"My manager thinks so."

"Oh, tell me about it!" Savannah squealed.

"I can't really. Until we get the contract signed with the publisher, I can't talk about it. I can tell you it's about a fire that destroyed a town."

"Oh... like the Willowcreek fire years ago? You know Carter lost his parents in that fire."

"Yeah, I know. I tried to get him to tell me about it, but he won't talk about it."

"That's something he won't talk about with anybody. Not ever."

"I've learned that."

"Well when do you think it'll be coming out?"

"I'm not sure yet. There's a lot of details I have to iron out with my manager."

"Well, now that you've got your book, are you staying around or are you going back out to Hollywood?"

Lily laughed. "Not everyone in the film industry lives in Hollywood. I much prefer Texas or Arizona. I'm not sure what I'm going to do. I'm still searching for the answer to that." Her own words suddenly made her remember what Susan had said: 'Everybody's searchin' for something when they come here.'

The narrow trail ended and opened up into a wide expanse of green grass with a large concrete building on the other side.

"That's the arena. I'd say they're pretty close to starting. You might want to head on over there if you're ready to run."

"Yeah, I guess so."

"Good luck on your run."

Lily smiled. "Thanks, Savannah."

Lily watched as the younger woman rode off toward the outdoor pen. Although she had dreaded getting into a conversation with Savannah, she actually wound up enjoying talking with her.

She made her way down the hill to the entrance of the indoor pen. As she reined Mercado through the wide entrance, she scanned the sea of riders, absently looking for Carter. She didn't see him anywhere and breathed a sigh of relief mixed with disappointment.

She found an open spot on the rail outside of the pen and stepped off of Mercado. The tractor driver was dragging the arena so she knew she still had a few more minutes before the actual race would start. She pulled her phone from its holder on her belt and checked her messages. Nate had texted that he had made it to the hotel, was going to eat and then would meet with the producer. Hopefully she wouldn't get the call from Nate until after she ran and had plenty of time. She needed to focus on her run. If her practice run was any indication, she needed all the focus she could get.

She checked her cinch and found it had loosened. She untied the knot and gave the strap a good tug upward to take out the slack and tied it back. She busied herself with double checking her breast collar and bridle making sure all the loops were tucked, buckles done, and all the leather secure. One thing she had learned when it came to horsemanship was to check your equipment. If a strap broke or a buckle came undone in the middle of running it could be disastrous.

Next, she re-strapped Mercado's bell boots and splint boots and then picked out his feet. It was a ritual she'd developed over time and it always seem to help her calm down before her run and focus.

A few minutes later, the tractor driver finished smoothing the arena and the announcement was made that they were starting the race. Lily's heart rate jumped in reaction.

She took a deep breath and decided she'd better send Nate a text to let him know she would be running within the next thirty minutes. Hopefully he wouldn't need her before then. With shaking hands, she sent him a quick test to which he just replied, "Okay."

She led Mercado towards the holding pen at the far end of the arena. She wanted to get in the holding pen as soon as this set finished running.

Although she wanted to watch the competition to see what she was up against, she forced herself not to watch. She didn't want the image of a knocked barrel or bad run in her mind when she was trying so hard to focus on a good run. It really was a mental game for her.

She fingered the braids she'd put in the gelding's mane as she waited for this set of riders to finish running.

Finally, the announcer announced the next set of riders, of which Lillie Starr was listed. Again, her heart leapt as she heard her writer name called. She could still kick herself for not signing up with her real name. She hoped Savannah was the only one that recognized the name.

She gathered her reins and went to mount up when she saw Carter ride by on the other side of the walkway. She really didn't want him watching her run, but she knew there was nothing she could do about it unless she just turned out. She wouldn't give him that satisfaction, but she knew him well and knew he would be picking her run apart.

He flashed her that magnetic smile and told her "Good luck."

Trying her best to keep up a cold front, she told him, "Thanks."

She took a deep breath and rode to the holding pen while the sound of the tractor filled the building.

She walked Mercado in little circles in the corner while the eight other riders entered the pen. He was well warmed up and relaxed which made her more confident. She was the third runner in this set which gave her a few minutes to settle and gather her thoughts before she had to run. As before, she didn't watch but kept her mind focused on her run and her gelding.

Finally, she heard her name and it was time to go. She took a deep breath, gathered her reins and pushed her heels down. She knew Mercado would be even stronger this run and this time she was ready for it.

She reined the dancing gelding towards the alley way and took him down the far wall to get him lined up for first. She felt the enormous power just below the surface and knew that when she released the reins, she'd better be ready to go.

Halfway down the alley, she pushed her hands forward and the gelding sprung forward in one giant leap. This time, Lily was right in time with him and stayed right where she needed to be.

She dropped her outside rein and grabbed the horn as she steered the gelding into the first barrel with the inside rein. The approach was spot-on, and the pair skimmed around the barrel in a flawless turn and it felt good.

Mercado blasted off the barrel with Lily up in the saddle. The pair lined up for the second barrel. With a perfect pocket, the gelding made the tight turn in one smooth move before rocketing off and heading for third.

By this time, several riders including Carter were watching the fast, smooth run. Carter pulled his horse over to the rail and climbed up on the fence to get a better view. It seemed the cowgirl knew how to run after all.

Mercado approached third at a blinding speed, and Lily was ready as she set him up for the turn. As he started to turn on the back side of the last barrel, the ground gave way, his feet slipping out sideways underneath him. The crowd gasped as the gelding slammed to the ground on his side, still desperately trying to keep his feet underneath him.

Lily was launched forward in the process, her head banging against the edge of the metal rim as she fell. The world went black as her palomino gelding fought to get to his feet and then trotted off towards the gate.

"Close the gate!" Carter yelled at the top of his lungs as he leapt from the fence and raced across the arena towards Lily's limp body.

Lily was lying on her back in the deep dirt, next to the barrel and bright red blood was gushing from the large gash on her forehead.

"Lily...Lily." Carter gently shook her by the shoulder but there was no response.

A tall older man rushed up and handed him some clean gauze from an emergency kit. "Tracy already called 911. They're on their way. They said not to move her unless absolutely necessary in case she had a neck injury. Just keep her still."

Carter nodded and knelt down beside Lily and covered the cut with the gauze and kept slight pressure on it to stem the bleeding. His hands shook as he wiped the dirt off of her face with his free hand.

In moments, they were surrounded by curious onlookers, all mumbling questions about who she was, what had happened, and comments about how good the run had been up until that point and how hard she had fallen. With the stress and worry, their comments made Carter feel a bit claustrophobic.

"Can everyone just step back?" he snapped. The older man ushered people back while Carter stayed at Lily's side and then knelt down beside them both.

"You know her?" the older man asked.

"Yeah. we've been kind of seeing each other. Her name is Lily Perkins. She's an author, writes under the name Lillie Starr."

"I thought she was new."

"Yeah, she moved her a couple months ago from out west. This was her first time running here…. She doesn't have anybody else." He pushed the tears back and looked at the older man. "I didn't realize it until now, but she means more to me than anything and I was too proud and stupid to let her know that."

The older man smiled wistfully. "You'll get the chance to tell her. You will."

"I hope so. God, I hope so."

Carter sank into the dirt and gently stroked Lily's cheek as he waited for the emergency workers to get there. He had the chance to tell her he was sorry at least twice today and he didn't and now he risked losing her forever. If anything happened to her, he could never forgive himself. The fire had hurt him more deeply than he ever thought possible, but this was even worse.

A few moments later a pair of emergency workers came running up with a board and Carter stepped back to let them work. As the woman started taking vitals, she asked Carter for her patient's name and age and whether or not she had any next of kin.

"Lily Perkins, she's 35. Can I go with you to the hospital?"

"Sorry, only family can go. They'll probably want to life flight her out of here with a head injury and her being unconscious. Any next of kin?"

"Me, I'm her husband." Carter blurted out.

Several of the people within earshot that knew him gave Carter a strange look so he added, "We just got married...a day ago. Newlyweds."

"Mister Perkins, you'll want to bring what information you can to the hospital."

"Shelton. She didn't change her name."

"Helicopter will be here in just a few. Let's go ahead and get her out to the parking lot."

Carter watched as the workers transferred Lily to the board. As they did, her phone fell out of her back pocket. The worker picked it up and handed it to Carter who quickly put it in his shirt pocket.

By the time the workers brought Lily to the parking lot, the helicopter had already landed and was ready to go. Carter watched in silence as they lifted Lily into the helicopter and then took off heading east.

"Mr. Shelton, they're taking her to UT Hospital."

Carter nodded and told them "Thanks" as he suddenly remembered Lily's horse and headed back inside.

He saw the palomino gelding just inside next to the fence. Savannah was holding the reins.

"She going to be okay?" she asked.

"I hope so. She cut her forehead pretty bad. I need to get to the hospital, Savannah."

"Go, I'll make sure everything gets taken care of."

"I'm going to unhook my truck and leave my trailer here."

"Alright. I'll make sure this guy and your horse gets home. Don't worry."

Carter gave her a quick hug. "Thanks."

He found Lily's purse in her truck, and then proceeded to unhook his truck from his trailer. He made it to the hospital in record time, found a parking place and then made his way to the information desk.

"Lily Perkins," he told the woman at the desk.

"What's your relationship?"

"Her husband."

"Okay, Mr. Perkins, I need you to fill out this paperwork."

"Shelton, she kept her maiden name. Do you know how she is?" he asked as he took the clip board and pen.

"All I can tell you is that she's in ICU. I don't know anything further Mr. Shelton. Once you get the paperwork filled out, go through those double doors and take a left down the hall to the main desk. You can find out how she's doing."

Carter numbly found a chair and started filling out the forms that the woman had handed him. Thankfully, he had all the information from Lily's purse that he needed. He quickly completed the forms and then handed them back to the woman at the desk and then went through the double doors.

He walked up to the central desk that was banked by a circle of patient slots.

"Who are you here for?"

"Lily Perkins."

"What's your relationship?"

"Her husband."

"Have a seat in the waiting area. One of the nurses will be there in a moment to give you an update."

Carter was the only one in the waiting area. He had too much energy, and thoughts to sit down and instead paced back and forth by the window.

He could kick himself for not telling her how he felt. He never would have guessed she would have gotten hurt like this. There was always a risk riding horses, and especially with barrel racing, but it always happened to someone else. Why did it have to be Lily? He hoped she would be awake. That would be a good sign, right?

The double doors burst open and a small Asian woman stepped through. "Mr. Perkins?"

"Mr. Shelton. Lily kept her maiden name. How is she?"

The woman held out her hand. "I'm Doctor Townsend. Well, she's lucky to be alive at this point and we're doing everything we can do."

Carter shook her hand. "What do you mean?"

"From the cut on her head and the way the accident happened, she's lucky she didn't fracture her cervical vertebra." Seeing the confused look on Carter's face, she added, "Break her neck."

She ushered Carter over to one of the chairs and motioned for him to sit down as she continued. "We did an MRI of her neck and skull. The neck, as I said before was clean, but she has a concussion with a brain bleed. Especially since she's not conscious, the next twenty-four to forty-eight hours are critical. I'll take you to see her in a moment but, Mr. Shelton, you need to understand these things can go either way and even when they turn out good, it's a long haul."

Carter nodded in silence as he took in what the petite doctor had to say. He followed out to a far patient slot at the far end of the main room. As she pulled back the curtain, Carter's eyes were drawn to Lily. Her color was so pale, and she was hooked up to IV's and monitors.

Dr. Townsend looked at her watch. "Visiting hours are until 9pm so you have a couple of hours. After that, you're welcome to stay in the family waiting area where we were earlier. The chairs pull out for sleeping and there's a shower in the restroom. You might as well settle in."

"You think she can hear me?'

Dr. Townsend smiled, "I like to think so, at least on some level. Talk to her. It helps."

As she turned to leave, Carter pulled the chair next to the bed and sat down and gently rubbed Lily's arm. "God, it kills me to see you like this," he told her quietly.

"I'm so, so sorry Lily. I'm so sorry I hurt you. I never meant those words I said to you. You do belong, with me. I need you. I haven't been able to think about anything else but you. I've been miserable. I need you in my life. I love you."

He watched her closely for any sign of movement from her, but the only movement was the lines on the heart monitor.

He reached up and smoothed the hair back from her face and gently kissed her cheek. "God, I need you."

He spent the next hour and a half holding on to Lily's arm and stroking her soft skin. He never wanted to leave her side ever again.

"Mr. Shelton, visiting hours are ending," the nurse said quietly as she pulled the curtain back.

Carter nodded and stood up. He bent over and kissed Lily on the cheek again, "Well, babe, I've got to go for now, but I won't be far away. I love you."

He rubbed her arm one last time and turned to leave. It tugged on his heart strings to have to leave her for even a little while. He knew he wasn't far away, but that still didn't make it any easier.

He found a comfortable chair in the waiting room and grabbed the TV remote. He blindly flipped through the channels, not really paying attention as his mind was rolling over the day's events.

Suddenly he felt a buzzing in his pocket. It was Lily's phone.

"Where the hell have you been? I've been trying to reach you for hours."

"Who is this?"

"Nate. Where the hell is Lily? I need to talk to her as soon as possible. She was supposed to answer earlier."

Carter sighed. "Lily's had an accident."

"Oh my God...is she...is she okay?"

"At this point I don't know. She's unconscious. Her horse fell when she was running barrels and she hit her head on the barrel. She's got a brain bleed and concussion."

"What hospital is she in?"

"She's in UT Hospital, in Knoxville," Carter told him.

"I'll be there as soon as I can." Nate said and then hung up.

"Well okay then," Carter said to the phone.

He suddenly realized he needed to call Susan and let her know what had happened. He pulled out his phone and dialed the number.

"Hey Susan, it's Carter."

"Hey Carter, what are you doing calling this late? What's wrong? Is everything okay?"

"No Susan...No, it's not."

"Oh Lord...what's happened?" He could hear the panic in her voice.

"It's Lily. Her horse fell while she was running, and she hit her head on the barrel. She's unconscious and has a brain bleed. She's in UT Hospital."

"I'll be up there first thing in the morning. Poor girl doesn't have anybody. She shouldn't be alone during something like this."

"She's got me," Carter replied a bit too defensively.

"Does she, Carter? Really have you?"

"I love her, Susan," Carter told her softly.

"I know. I know you do. Okay, I'll be up there by eight in the morning, alright?"

"Okay."

"You holding up? You need me to bring you anything? Food, change of clothes, a beer?"

He laughed. "Thanks. A change of clothes would be good. I don't feel much like eating. Too worried to eat. I can't lose her. Not now."

"I know. I'll bring you what you need. See you in the morning."

"Thanks. See you later."

Chapter Fourteen

Carter jerked awake in the morning light at the sound of a door opening. He rubbed at his blurry eyes and sat up.

"Sorry to wake you up." Susan said quietly. "You look rough."

"Hell, I feel rough. These chairs aren't the most comfortable, but I guess it's better than staying down the road."

"Any updates?"

"I haven't been in there yet." He glanced at his watch. "Visiting hours just started about thirty minutes ago. You want to go in and see her?"

"Yeah. You want to get cleaned up first? I stopped by your place and grabbed your toothbrush and some toothpaste, razor and all that." She handed him the small black bag.

"Thanks. I'll only be a couple of minutes."

He dashed into the small bathroom and turned on the water. He almost didn't recognize the man in the mirror. He quickly brushed his teeth and freshened up. He didn't want to waste any more time. He wanted to see Lily.

Susan followed Carter past the central nurse's station to Lily's bed. She held her breath as Carter pulled the curtain back and they stepped up to the bed.

"Hey baby, I'm back," Carter told Lily quietly as he stepped up to the bed and rubbed her arm. "Susan's here to see you too." He nodded at Susan. "You can tell her hello. The doctor says she might hear."

"Hey Lily," Susan said hesitantly. Truth be told, she felt a little strange talking to Lily without any response.

"The doctor said the next twenty-four to forty-eight hours are pretty important. She's just been sleeping like this."

"Well, she'll wake up soon, Carter. Just have hope."

"Yeah. She's got to wake up. I have to tell her I'm sorry."

"What do you mean? You two have a fight?"

"Yeah, and I was an ass. The book she was writing was about the fire, and she asked me about it and I mouthed off. You know I don't like talking about that. Then she had a key of my mother's and I just lost it. She tried to give it back, but I didn't want the damn thing, told her that what we had between us hadn't meant anything. I screwed up big time, Susan, and now I'm worried I can't fix it... She's all I've been able to think about."

Susan rubbed his back. "I know. I know you love her. I could tell that a long time ago with the way you got upset."

"I have never loved anybody like I love her. Ever."

"Carter, all you can do is wait."

"I know... I just feel helpless."

One of the nurses stopped by the end of the bed. "Good morning. How's your wife doing this morning?"

"Wife?" Susan gasped.

Carter gave her a funny look and then answered, "Oh, my wife is about the same. First time I've been able to get a word in edgewise. You know how women are..."

As the nurse shook her head and then stepped forward to check Lily's heart monitor and IV, Carter put his finger up to his lips behind her back to signal Susan to be quiet. Neither of them said anything as the nurse typed in her notes on the iPad and left.

"What the hell was that all about, Carter?" Susan hissed. "Wife? Did you go get married? Oh, good Lord..."

"No, no it's not what you think. When the EMTS came to get her yesterday, they said that only family could go with her to the hospital, so without thinking I blurted out that I was her husband and that we'd just gotten married."

Susan breathed a sigh of relief. "You had me worried, although as bad as you have it for her, it really wouldn't surprise me in the least."

"You think she cares for me Susan? I think she does some, I'm just not sure she cares enough to stay, especially if she sold this latest book. There's nothing to keep her here."

"Nothing but you and that might be enough." She hesitated for a moment and then continued. "Carter, you want me to tell you what I really think?"

"You've never held back before."

"No, Carter I haven't always told you everything I knew or thought, but this time I am."

"Well, go ahead."

"Both of you have been hurt really bad. You've put up walls so high nobody can get in, not really. You're so used to losing people that you never really let your guard down. You're searching for someone to call home, but you never become vulnerable enough to let that happen so that when it all falls apart, you don't get hurt. That works for a while, but how is that going to work thirty years from now when you're getting to the end of your life? The nights get awfully lonely when you get old. Trust me, I know. If you really love her, let your pride go, let those walls go and give it all you've got. Love her with everything you have."

"I can't help but do that, Susan. I've fought it this entire time and I can't help but love her more than life itself."

"That's good to hear. I know it may not seem like it at the moment, but it takes love to get through things like this. At least you've felt love, true love, once in your life."

"Mr. Shelton, I'm Doctor Finch." The younger man stepped forward and shook Carter's hand. "I've been reviewing Lily's chart and test results this morning. We're going to take her down here in a little bit for some more tests to make sure she's not developing any swelling on her brain and to see if that small bleed has resolved with the medication."

"Is she any better?"

Dr. Finch shined the light into Lily's eyes checking her pupils. "Hard to say. From everything we're seeing she should be awake. Her pupils are reacting, which is good. We just don't quite know why she's not waking up and responding at the moment."

"How long can she stay like this?"

"We don't know. She may wake up in five minutes or ten years. We just simply don't know everything about these brain injuries." He made some notes and then added, "They'll be up in about twenty minutes to take her for testing. You might want to go down and get some breakfast. They have a great breakfast buffet. You need to keep your strength up."

"Will do."

Carter sat down beside the bed and held Lily's hand. He nor Susan said a word, just sat there in the silence, each lost in their own thoughts.

A little while later an aide came to take Lily down for her tests. Carter and Susan watched as they rolled her down the hallway and then headed to get breakfast. Strong coffee and some scrambled eggs would hit the spot.

Carter and Susan made small talk about cattle prices, hay and the local Willowcreek livestock sale gossip while they ate. Anything to keep Carter's mind off of Lily for a little while.

As they walked back in the room, the aide was locking Lily's bed into place.

"I'm going to go ahead and go." Susan reached and gave Carter a hug. "Holler at me if you need anything, okay?"

He nodded and then added, "Thank you, Susan, for the talk…and just for everything."

"Carter, hang in there. It's going to be alright."

"I hope so. I can't lose her."

He watched as Susan left and then settled onto the edge of the padded chair next to Lily's bed. He smoothed back her hair and kissed her soft cheek. "Lily baby, you need to wake up. I need you. I don't like saying that, but I do. I didn't realize it until now."

For a long time, he sat just rubbing Lily's arm and staring at her, taking in every single curve and line of her face. He would give anything to hear her wake up and talk.

After a while, his eyes became heavy and he fell asleep in the chair beside Lily's bed.

"Oh my God…Lily."

Carter jerked awake to see a tall, fit man with salt and pepper hair standing at the end of Lily's bed. He jumped to his feet. "Who are you?"

"You must be Carter. I'm Nate, Lily's manager. Any change?"

Carter rubbed his eyes and shook his head no.

Nate walked to the other side of the bed and grabbed Lily's hand as he bent over and kissed the top of her head. "Lil, it's Nate. I'm here, sweetie. I made it."

"What have the doctors said?"

"Not a whole lot, except that the next couple of days are critical for her to wake up."

"So, they can't tell you if she'll wake up?"

Carter stood up and changed the subject. "You two must be pretty close for you to drop everything and come all the way to Tennessee."

Nate pulled a chair up beside Lily. "You could say that."

Carter stiffened. "She didn't really talk about you a whole lot, just that you were her manager."

"We've worked together for several years now. We talk pretty much every single day, especially when she's working on a project, but we have never actually met face to face." He squeezed Lily's hand and added, "Now is as good of a time as ever I guess, huh Lil?"

Carter sat down and strummed his fingers on the edge of his chair as he watched the slightly older man gazing at the woman he suddenly felt the need to fight for. "Lily never said if you were married."

Carter's comment jerked Nate's attention back to reality "Ummm, yes technically I am."

"What do you mean *technically*?" Carter pressed.

"Well, I hadn't told Lily, but my wife and I are separated. I told her about a month ago I wanted a divorce and she left shortly after. I didn't want to mention it to Lily, just yet."

Carter leaned back against the door frame and looked Nate in the eye. "I see. When were you going to mention it?'

Nate shifted awkwardly in his seat. "Well, I know that you two have been seeing each other…"

"Mr. Shelton, I'm here to check on your wife and get her vitals."

Carter leered at Nate as he stepped to the side to let the nurse through.

"My name is Melissa and I'll be checking on her the rest of this afternoon if you need anything." she told them as she checked the heart monitor and IV.

Carter never took his eyes off of Nate and noted the look of disappointment behind his professional façade. Neither man said a word as the nurse did her routine and then bid goodbye, telling Carter to get her if his wife needed anything.

"Lily didn't tell me…I guess it's more serious than I realized. And quick. Well, maybe not for Lily. She does tend to be impetuous."

"Yeah, things happened rather quickly between us. You didn't have plans…"

"For Lily? Oh no… no…. no. I uh…. Well, she's a client and that's never a good idea."

"A writer and her agent? Seems like that would be the perfect match. So why not?" Carter was enjoying seeing the other man squirm.

"It's just well known in the industry. Besides, with her having a movie coming up it wouldn't have been a good time anyhow."

"A movie?"

"She didn't tell you before she had the accident?"

"No, we were both kind of busy before she ran."

"Hmmm." Nate cocked his head to the side. "That's strange. Busy or not, that's something Lily would have been shouting to the rooftops. She's waited so long to have another hit, I wouldn't think that's something that she'd keep to herself easily."

Carter shifted uncomfortably against the door just as Dr. Finch stepped into the room.

"Well hello, Mr. Shelton."

Carter stepped up and shook the doctor's hand. "How are you?"

"Not half bad. This is the end of my rounds for the day and I'll be getting ready to head out. I just wanted to stop in for a moment and check on your wife"

The two men caught each other's eyes for a split second.

"And who is this gentleman?"

"Nate. Nate Kinsley. I'm Lily's managing agent."

"Agent?" The doctor turned and looked questioningly at Carter.

"Well yes," Nick piped up. "She's an author. Well, and screenwriter as well. Didn't Carter tell you?" Nate smiled wickedly at Carter as he added, "Yes, she's written several movies. The last one was her biggest, Always and Forever."

"Oh yeah! I've seen that movie. My wife absolutely loved it."

"Charming! I tell you what Doc, get this wonderful woman well and I'll make sure she signs a copy of her book just for your wife. How's that?"

Dr. Finch laughed. "That's a plan."

"So, what's the latest? How's she doing and when is she going to get out of here?"

Dr. Finch hesitated and looked at Carter, who sighed and nodded. "Well, I guess I'll tell you both then. Her brain bleed has resolved according to the CT scan we did this morning."

"That's good."

"It is good, very good. There doesn't appear to be any swelling." He told them both as he stepped to the side of Lily's bed. "I'll check her pupils."

Neither man said a word as they watched the doctor separate Lily's eyelids and shine the light in each eye. "Her pupils are reacting to light, so that's good."

"So why isn't she awake?" Nate asked rather impatiently.

"That we don't know."

Nate sighed, "I hate to say it but had this been New York or Chicago, she probably would have been conscious by now. They have cutting edge technology there and the top specialists. Maybe we need to move her there."

"Mr. Kinsley, I can understand your frustration. However, even if this is little ol' Tennessee this is a level one trauma center and we have great specialists and technology. She's getting excellent care, I can assure you."

"She should have already opened her eyes and…"

Dr. Finch nodded, "I agree. There's nothing on her CT that indicated she should be unconscious, but that's just how the brain works. We've seen CT scans that the patient shouldn't have been alive, and they were talking and functioning fine. And we've seen plenty more CT scans that indicated a perfectly healthy brain and they weren't conscious for years. CT scans are just a tool to see what's going on. You're barely twenty-four hours in right now. You still have time."

"Time?" Carter asked.

Dr. Finch turned to talk to him directly. "Yes. After a few days, the chances of their coming out of the coma goes down. The longer they're unconscious, the more likely they'll stay that way long term."

Nate let out a large sigh and impatiently plopped down in the chair.

"I'll be in tomorrow afternoon to check on her. Dr. Townsend is covering another shift and she'll probably be in in a little while," he told them as he made notes on his iPad.

"Thanks doc," Carter said quietly.

Dr. Finch smiled wistfully. "No problem. Hang in there."

Carter nodded and stepped aside as Dr. Finch left.

"She needs to be moved," Nate said tersely.

"This is a good hospital. One of the best in the Southeast."

"Come on, this little one-horse town?" Nate hissed.

"Look, I'm not a doctor or an Einstein. I'm just a simple cowboy."

"Yeah, just like she always chases..." The vicious words slipped out unheeded.

"Oh... so that's what this is about. I may be simple, but I wasn't born in a turnip patch, and it damn sure wasn't last night."

"What the hell is *that* supposed to mean?"

"You're the big high society educated *agent*. You tell me. You just want her for yourself. That's the only reason you want to move her."

"I just want the best for Lily. You don't seem to be too worried about her and she's your wife... or is she?"

"Of course she's my wife, and I want what's best for her and she should be here with me!"

Hearing the commotion from the nurse's station, one of the nurses rushed into the room. "Gentleman, you need to take this discussion elsewhere. She doesn't need to hear this, and neither do the rest of us! Out!" she hissed as she pointed to the hallway.

Carter shook his head. "It's okay, I'm going. He can... he can stay here."

"Visiting hours will be over in about an hour. I suggest that you two either visit her separately or resolve your issue before you come back or you won't be allowed in here. Understand?"

Like scolded children, both men nodded and then Carter headed to the waiting room. He pushed open the door a little harder than he realized, and it banged against the wall. He glanced at the nurses who were scowling at the desk and said, "Sorry."

He walked to the window and looked out. All he could see was a courtyard below. He'd give anything to be at the top of one of the hills on the farm, watching the sun go down into the purple and blue haze. Suddenly the four walls around him were closing in and he felt much like a caged animal with nowhere to go.

He paced back and forth as he thought about Nate and why he had shown up there. It was clear Nate wanted Lily and that's what he came here for even though he knew she had been seeing Carter. He wondered what had caused Nate's breakup. Had he dumped his wife for Lily? Married five times or not, Lily deserved better than that!

At the same time, he also knew she deserved better than a cowboy as messed up as he was. She needed more, someone that would love her no matter what and appreciate her for who she was.

While he couldn't vouch for whether or not Nate would love her no matter what, he could vouch for the fact that Nate fully appreciated her. That part was obvious. It was undeniable that he highly respected her as a writer, and that part was where Carter fell short. He would never be the intellect on the level that Nate was. He was much simpler than that. Even if Lily did wake up and they resolved their differences, now he wondered if he'd ever be enough for her.

The door opened, and Nate stepped through. He pointed back behind him and said, "They're cleaning her up for the night."

Carter stopped pacing and sat down in the oversize chair by the window. He pretended to be looking into the courtyard between the buildings, but truthfully he didn't see a thing as his mind was turbulent with thoughts of the man right across from him.

Nate stood at the window just a few feet away, searching for something to say but words failed him. Instead he grabbed the remote from the small table by the wall, found a ball game on the TV and sat down on the large couch across the room. The game was a welcome break from the tension in the room, but it was only temporary as the game ended just a few minutes later.

Nate fidgeted as he scrolled through the channels looking for something to watch. Nothing caught his interest, so he turned the television off. He sighed and sat forward on the couch.

He cleared his voice and then said, "So tell me something, Carter."

"Geez…here we go." Carter mumbled as he shook his head.

"If she comes out of this alright, and I'm hoping that she does, how are you going to take care of her if she has some handicap and needs care?"

"What is it with the deep questions here, like it's any of your business anyhow!"

"Well, answer the question. Someone has to for her sake and keep your voice down. I'm sure you don't want to get thrown out of here anymore than I do."

"I don't know…. Shoe more horses, I guess? Take on a second job. Whatever I have to do if it comes to that."

"I see…you're one of those that lives for today, doesn't give a shit about tomorrow."

"Now wait a minute!"

"It's true. And it's true that you wouldn't be able to take care of her or give her what she needs."

"You don't know that."

"No, but I know Lil and I know she's had enough of the bottom falling out on her and she's tired of it. She needs stability, someone to take care of her even if she does play the strong cowgirl who can do it all on her own."

"Who's to say I can't give that? You don't know anything about me."

"No, but I know your type. I've seen it before, more than once with her."

"And just what is my type, Nate?"

"The cowboy that's only there for a good time. When the new wears off, you're gone."

Carter's face turned red as he bolted out the door, leaving Nate's mocking chuckle behind. He had to get away. His own heartbeat was ringing in his ears as the anger pulsed through his veins. On one hand he wanted to jerk the suave prick up by his neck and slam him out the window to the courtyard below. On the other hand, he was right, and the words stung harder than they should have.

What the hell was he doing here, acting like a husband who would be committed the rest of his life to a woman he didn't know all that well but loved more than anything? This wasn't like him. He *was* the man that Nate said he was. As George Strait's song said, he wasn't here for a long time, just here for a good time.

Or was he? God, he was so confused! He had just been reacting this whole entire time to the whim of his feelings and damn Nate had to ask the hard questions, the ones where he hadn't thought that far, the ones that made reality come crashing in.

He knew he felt something for Lily he hadn't ever felt before. She'd gotten under his skin and gave him a run for his money unlike any woman he'd ever met. He couldn't wrap her around his little finger like all the others. She was fire and ice, had a mind of her own and the wildness of a young horse, and when she wasn't around the world was a dark and quiet place that he just couldn't handle.

After walking around for a half hour or so, he found a bench in a hallway and sat down, running his hands through his wavy hair. He sat there for a few minutes when an older man that looked to be in his eighties walked up to the bench.

He let out a big breath as he sat down, "I just have to sit for a moment. I'm out of breath. It's a long way from that parking garage."

Carter half smiled and nodded. "Yes sir, it is."

"I'm here to see my wife. She's been in the hospital for a week now."

"I'm sorry to hear that."

The older man nodded. "Thank ya. It's been hard. We're hoping she'll get released to the nursing home the next few days. She had a stroke. She's trying, I can see it in her eyes."

"Well I bet she is." Carter encouraged him.

"Been married for over sixty years. Can't give up now."

"Wow... that's a long time. How'd you know she was the one?"

"Awww son, I didn't know. I just knew I couldn't see myself without her. She's been everything to me."

"I can tell you love her."

"I do, always have through the good and the bad. Just couldn't help it."

"I can understand that." He couldn't help but love Lily. He'd tried his best not to.

The older man looked at his watch and then said, "Well, I guess I'd better go now that I've caught my breath." He winked at Carter and added, "She'll be waiting on me for supper and she's not very patient."

"Well, you'd better get up there."

"Yep. Good talkin' to ya."

Carter watched the old man go down the hallway and thought about their conversation. It was a sign, he was sure of it.

When Carter made it back to the waiting room, he breathed a sigh of relief to find it empty and Nate nowhere in sight. He was glad to have a little peace and quiet as he came to terms with what was happening.

He loved Lily, period. The old man in the hallway had shown him that. If she didn't wake up, that wouldn't change but he'd have to find a way to deal with it.

If she did wake up, well, he had another dilemma on his hands – who would she choose once she found out that Nate had feelings for her? So far he'd been his usual cocky self, just knowing that it would be him. But there was a chance it might not be since she had a history with Nate and Nate offered stability and familiarity, and probably more money.

Just imagining Lily choosing Nate turned his stomach. He couldn't let that happen, no matter what. It had to be him and nobody else, ever. He'd made his mind up.

Chapter Fifteen

Carter woke up just as the sky was starting to turn orange. Although the couch had been adequately comfortable and the room quiet, he had tossed relentlessly the entire night with thoughts of Lily choosing Nick over him.

He had just stood up when Nate came through the door.

"I'm going to get coffee." Carter said blandly.

"Oh, I figured you'd need some." He held a cup out, "Starbucks."

He was a tad bit too chipper, nonetheless causing Carter to tilt his head and smile slightly. "I've never had Starbucks in my whole life. That shit's too expensive."

Nate smiled slyly as he hovered over his own hot cup. "I figured it's the least I can do since I'm going to wind up with Lily."

A nerve worked back and forth in Carter's jaw but he kept his tongue in check. "We'll just see about that."

"Look, I thought about this last night. In fact, it was all I could think about. You are Lily's usual type, I'll give you that, but Lily is looking for a change. She's looking for stability and someone that's going to see her through the long haul – especially if she comes out of this with any issues. I'm more prepared for that reality than you are. She could be paralyzed for all we know…"

"Hell, you're headed for a divorce. You don't know what you're prepared for until that's all said and done." Carter sat down and took a sip of the hot coffee. As the dark, bitter taste hit his tongue it tasted good, but hell would freeze over before he let his rival know that.

He continued, "You don't really know that much about me, Nate." He smirked. "Yeah, she might have told you I was hot, but other than that you don't know a damn thing about me. What I do or how I do it."

Nate nodded slightly, "You're right, I'm going primarily off the very small bit of information that Lily gave me, and a lot of assumptions. I've seen your type before."

"Well, my type – whatever that is - owns a large farm that I inherited from my family. My mother died in a fire, my father he died a few days later, mainly because he never got over her. I farm and I shoe horses. Now, in your nice little corporate business world, that might not seem like a whole lot of stability, but it's stability that doesn't walk away when the going gets tough."

A young dark headed nurse busted through the door, interfering with Nate's potential come back, "I hate to interrupt gentleman, but Lily's awake!"

Carter bolted by the nurse who promptly grabbed him. "Wait!" With a lot of effort, she steered him back into the room. "You can't go in there yet. I know you want to but the doctor on call is checking her vital signs and we don't want to overwhelm her as she's coming out of the coma."

"I need to see her…I need to tell her." He told her with his hand still on the door.

"I understand, Mister Shelton." She moved his hand off the door. "Just give us a few minutes for the doctor to check her out and then we'll let one of you go in when that's done." She gave Nate who had been silent and still an apologetic look. "You two will have to figure out who goes in there first." She put a hand on Carter's shoulder and ushered him to the couch in the corner. "Just have a seat and enjoy that hot cup of Starbucks. I didn't get any myself this morning." She told him.

Carter grudgingly sat down on the edge of the couch and took a mindless sip of his coffee. It burnt his tongue and he winced.

"Coffee's hot."

"No shit, Sherlock."

"You're the one that took a big gulp of it. Calm down," Nate chided.

"I need to be the first in there. I have to apologize and tell her I love her. At least let me do that...if you're going to whisk her off to New York City or wherever it is you live."

"Chicago. I live in Chicago."

Carter gave him a disapproving look. "Figures. You know, she may be a writer but she's a cowgirl at heart. She'll always have to have some wide open spaces to ride in. Some arena won't do for long."

"That's just a piece of her world. I can offer her more."

"Unless you're going to learn how to ride, you can't offer her a sunrise coming across the ridge above the fog from horseback, ...or making love on the front porch during a summer time rain."

Nate shifted his feet and rubbed his chin. "That's a little personal...Let's just wait...and see what the doctor says."

"Life is personal. You work with romance writers, you ought to be used to that kind of thing."

"Yeah, well writing fiction and hearing about your redneck fantasies are quite different."

Carter chuckled. The fact that he'd hit a nerve made the wait a little easier.

Both men sat in the waiting room in silence, each sipping their coffee. Nate checked emails and the latest news on his phone while Carter flipped mindlessly through channels on the television.

Carter hoped Lily would be okay. He knew that anything was possible, that she could potentially have some major health issues coming out of this and he tried not to imagine the worst case scenarios. He just wanted to be with her no matter what. He realized she was home to him. She was what made him smile and made him complete and he would do whatever it took for her to stay with him. She had to be his.

A few moments later a young doctor that barely looked sixteen came through the door. He looked perplexed at both men. "Mister Shelton?"

Carter stood. "Yes?"

The young doctor motioned for him to sit back down and sat down next to him on the couch.

"I'm Doctor Tillman. Lily is awake, and we have to do some testing later today…"

"How is she?" Nate interrupted.

The doctor looked at Nate and then back at Carter before responding. "Well, we won't know until the testing is complete, but she's awake. She's not sure what happened or how she got here. It's possible that the memory portions of her brain were impacted. We'll know more after the tests."

"How about her physical ability to move?" Nate asked.

Carter shot him an annoyed look.

"Well, she wanted to stand so we let her do that. She was a little unsteady on her feet, but she did fine. Again, we'll run an MRI to make sure but at least initially I'm not seeing any motor skill impairment at this time."

Carter let out the breath he'd been holding. "Oh, that's a relief!"

"You're a lucky man, Mister Shelton. This could have ended a lot worse."

He nodded, "I agree. So, can I go see her now?"

Doctor Tillman laughed. "Yeah, get in there."

Carter scrambled to his feet and busted through the door headed towards Lily's bed. The nurses jumped and scowled at him as he passed by the desk.

He scrunched his shoulders. "Sorry!" he whispered as he went by.

His heart was pounding in his chest as he neared Lily's bed. Her eyes were closed and although she had not stirred for the last forty-eight hours and her hair was a mess, he thought she was the most beautiful woman he'd ever seen. He stopped for just a moment and watched her in awe in the quiet. He was most definitely in love with this vibrant, smart mouthed cowgirl.

He sat down quietly by the bed and took a deep breath. "Lily...." He watched as her eyes fluttered open and then looked at him sleepily. "Hey..." He reached up and gently stroked her arm.

He wanted nothing more than to pull her to him and crush her with the weight of his embrace, but he figured that might not be the best approach – especially if there was a chance that she didn't remember who he was. After all, she could be pretty dang feisty, but then that's exactly what he loved about her.

Lily furrowed her brow and turned her head.

"Do you remember who I am?" he whispered, his hope hanging on every word.

Lily bit her lip and closed her eyes. "I...I..." She sighed in frustration.

"It's okay, you don't have to remember anything right this minute. I'm just glad you're awake."

"I'm thirsty. I...I need something to drink."

"I'll get it...Don't get up." He reached over and pushed the nurse call button.

"I don't want to sit here. I want to get up!" Lily snapped angrily as she swung her legs over the side of the bed.

"Nurse!" Carter wailed a little too loudly, causing Lily to jump.

One of the male nurses rushed in. "What's the problem?"

"She's wanting to get up and she can't do that!" Carter said.

The nurse stepped between Lily and Carter asking, "Why not? She's awake. She needs some help to make sure she's steady. Getting up would probably do her some good." He looked Lily in the eye and asked, "You ready to get up, little lady?"

Lily giggled and then nodded yes before pushing her feet to the floor and suddenly popping up.

"Easy there, let's do this slow. You've been down a couple of days. One step at a time. I don't want you to fall," the nurse told her as he kept a grip on her arm to keep her steady.

Lily closed her eyes as a wave of dizziness hit and she teetered back and forth.

"See, told you that would happen," he teased.

"Just give me a minute." She opened her eyes and leaned up to whisper in his ear. "Who is this handsome devil behind you? He seems familiar, but I'm not sure."

The young man chuckled and turned, "Oh that's Carter. Your husband."

"Uh… yeah," Carter replied sheepishly as he watched them.

"My husband? Me? Married? Are you sure?" Lily searched Carter's eyes and then shook her head. "Can't be." She sighed, trying to get her strength up. "Let me walk to the door and back."

"Alright," the patient young man told her.

Lily held onto his arm as she took a step towards the door, and then another. The dizziness was dissipating as she moved, but she still felt weak.

Keeping a supportive hand on his patient, the nurse turned and looked at Carter, "When we get to the door do you want to take over? She's pretty active - you may have to get used to this until she's moving better on her own."

"Are you sure? I mean…she doesn't even know who I am right now." Just saying the words hurt.

"What better way to get her memory back? Maybe the closeness…"

"Guys, I'm right here! He seems familiar, but I know myself well enough to know after the last fiasco, husband number…. oh hell, I can't remember but I know I wouldn't get married even if he is a good-looking cowboy!" She leaned around the nurse, "No offense, I mean you are a nice tall drink of water, but marriage and all… well, I don't do so well."

Carter just smiled and shook his head. It was good to see her spunk back even if she didn't know who he was. Maybe he was better off that she couldn't remember what he'd said to her. He might have to win her all over again. Come to think of it, that would be fun.

Lily reached the door and then turned to Carter who was now up and standing nearby. "You ready to take me for a spin?"

"Yeah, I guess so." He smiled.

"Don't get any ideas. I might like it too much," she quipped back as she took another careful step.

Carter blushed. "I don't know what to say to that."

"You don't have to, we're supposed to be married, remember?"

"So you're married now?" came a smooth voice from behind them both.

Lily spun around a little too quickly, causing her to shift off balance and fall against Carter. She recognized that voice. "Nate?"

Nate flashed Carter a look that would make the devil cringe. "Why yes!"

She straightened, pulling back somewhat from Carter. "What…what are you doing here?"

"Coming to check on my best author, of course."

"All the way from Chicago?"

Carter's pulse raced as he loosely held on to Lily. The fact that Lily couldn't remember him but clearly remembered everything about Nate hurt beyond words and the fact that the asshole was obviously reveling in her remembering didn't help matters.

Nate reached towards Lily and gave Carter a quick smile. "I think I can take it from here."

"You didn't have to come all this way to..." She stopped and furrowed her brow.

"Tennessee," Carter interjected.

"Yes, Tennessee. I'm in Tennessee." She sighed, "I can't remember the last few days, or what happened. The doctors just said that I had a bad fall barrel racing and hit my head."

"Well, that's why I came," Nate said softly.

"I'm going to get something to drink and leave you two...to talk." He shook his head and walked out.

"Carter, wait..." Something in her ached as she watched the play of emotions on his face as he left. He seemed more familiar, and memories played just at the edge of the fog in her head. She knew him, wanted him but that's all she knew.

"Nate, the nurse said that Carter was my husband. Is that true?"

He sighed, "That's what he told me and what the nurses said."

"Then why can't I remember him?" she asked, tears of panic welling up in her eyes. "I want to remember, and he seems familiar, but..."

"Don't worry about it. You'll remember." He patted her hand on his arm. "Let's get you back to bed."

"I think I can make it," she told him as she made the last few steps on her own and sat down on the edge of the bed.

"So really, why did you come all this way?" she asked as she settled back in the bed.

"Well, that's really a long story with a lot of reasons."

"Have you looked around? I think I've got time."

He chuckled, "Yes, you do." He sighed and took a seat in the chair by the bed. "Well, do you remember the story that you sent to me?"

She bit her lip as she thought for a moment. "Yeah…. You were waiting to hear back from the publisher is the last thing I remember."

He laughed, "Well, that's just the tip of the iceberg! You story hit it out of the park, Lil. They gave us a three-book deal and put us in touch with a television network executive. I met with the executive out in California the day you had your accident. They want to do a mini-series."

She squealed and clapped her hands, "You're kidding?"

"Nope, not at all." He leaned forward and took her hands in his and kissed them. "You were barrel racing, and I had agreed that I would call you while we were in the meeting. I called but you never answered. Then when Carter answered your phone, he told me what happened and I came straight here."

She smiled as she looked into his blue eyes and then suddenly remembered Jan. "Is Jan okay with your coming here?"

He suddenly let go of her hands and sat back. "That's the other reason I came. Jan left."

"Oh Nate, I'm so sorry. I thought you guys were good. I mean you always seemed like you got along so well."

"I did too, but she decided she wanted something else."

"You must be devastated."

"I am…but I'm not. If I was honest with myself, I knew it was coming. We got along but there was no passion, no fire…." He reached up an absently brushed the hair back from Lily's face.

"I'm so sorry."

"Thank you. It's just one of those things, but that's part of the reason I came here." He leaned over and took her hand. "I realize in all this how I feel about you."

She cocked her head to the side as she looked into his eyes. "Feel about me? What…what are you saying Nate?"

He jumped up and started pacing. "Oh hell, I had a whole speech planned out…I'm in love with you, Lily."

"Oh my God."

"Well damnit, that's not the reaction I was hoping for."

She closed her eyes and winced. "I don't…I don't know what to say."

"Of course not… you're just waking up from a coma. I'm such an idiot!"

She shook her head. "No, no you're not." She pleaded. "I just… I'm married…and this whole accident I can't remember much of anything. It's just too much!"

"I don't know that you're really married. I think Carter was just saying that," he confided.

"Why? Why would…what's his name? Carter? Why would he say we were married when we're not?"

"I don't know, but neither one of you have a ring and he just doesn't act like a man who has just married a famous author such as yourself." He reached over and absently wrapped a stray curl around his finger.

She shook her head. "There's a lot I can't remember, but somehow I know Carter wouldn't do that."

"Wouldn't do what?" Carter asked as he stepped into the room.

A flash of crimson went up both their cheeks as Nate tried to salvage the moment. "Ummm…"

"Oh hell, I'll just get right to the point. It's my life anyhow and God knows I couldn't screw it up any more if I tried." Lily quipped.

Carter flashed his best smile, "I wouldn't expect anything less, my dear."

"Nate here has left his wife and said he realizes he loves me. He also says he doesn't believe you and I are married, that you don't have a ring and don't act like a married person." Lily knew the answer the second she watched the color drain from his face. "Why? Why would you lie?"

Carter shook his head. "I had to. I had to know you were okay and they wouldn't tell me anything if I wasn't family."

"See, I told you," Nate sneered.

"Listen you son of..."

"Stop it, you two!" Lily yelled. She closed her eyes as the tears started to fall. "I can't remember... I need to remember."

Carter sat down on the edge of the bed and reached up to gently wipe Lily's tears. "Ssshhhh. You'll remember. It's going to be alright, and I'm not going anywhere, ever. I promise, I'm right here." He pulled her to him and wrapped his arms around her. "I love you and we'll work through this," he told her as she collapsed into his arms. The sound of her sobs hit a place within him that hadn't been touched since he was a child. He buried his face in her tousle of red hair.

Nate's jaw tensed as he stood by the door watching. His confession had backfired horribly and now it appeared he'd made the rushed trip in vain. He shook his head as he quietly stepped out of the room, leaving Lily's pain and his own pride behind.

Chapter Sixteen

Lily woke the next morning to find Carter still asleep in the chair by her bed. As she took in the chiseled features of the sleeping cowboy just out of reach, the memory of arguing with him danced at the edges of her mind.

Carter opened his eyes and then shuttered them against the sunlight streaming in. "Morning, Gorgeous." He gave her a boyish grin that made her heart spike just a bit.

"Good morning, Cowboy. How'd you sleep?"

"Not good, but that's okay. You're awake."

"Yeah…I remember an argument, but I don't remember much more. What were we arguing about?"

He laughed. "Which time?"

"Did we really argue that much?' she asked.

"Well, it wasn't a bed of roses. We're two peas in a pod when it comes to stubbornness."

"I remember it was something about a key…" She noticed the color drain from his cheeks.

He shook his head and leaned forward. "Look, you don't need to remember that. I….I wasn't too nice, and I'm sorry."

"I need to know. I don't want to blame you. I just want to put the pieces together."

He sighed. "It's just like you not to take the easy route."

"What cowgirl does?" she laughed.

"You've got a point."

"Before I tell you, just so you know, I tried to apologize to you before the barrel race."

"Ohhh…so you were feeling guilty." She nodded. "So that's why you lied about us being married. Guilt is a powerful thing, especially when you think someone is dead."

"Don't say that."

"It's true."

"I love you. That's why I lied."

"Love or guilt. Hmmm." she teased.

"You're not going to make this easy on me, are you. I just told you I love you."

"No, I'm not. Why were we arguing over the key?"

"Looking back, it was because I thought you were just after a story with the fire, but the truth is that you found something of my mother's I'd buried a long time ago."

She suddenly remembered how angry he would get whenever she mentioned the fire. "What is it about that fire that you're so defensive about? It doesn't make any sense."

He stood up and turned to look out the window and then closed his eyes. "Lily, there's some things about that fire I've never told anyone. Not Susan, not a soul." He ran his hands through his hair. "I started the fire. I didn't mean to, but I was somewhere I shouldn't have been."

"You were just a boy," Lily told him quietly.

"There's more."

"Okay."

"I skipped the afternoon at school and came home early. I heard something in the barn and went out to see what it was." He turned around and dropped back into the chair. "It was my mom." He sighed, "And Susan's husband. They were half dressed and making out in the barn loft. I saw him give her the key. I heard him say he was going to tell Susan that night. I panicked and ran, knocking over the heat lamp into the straw." He took a big breath, "That's what started the fire."

"Oh my God Carter… I had no idea," Lily whispered.

He shook his head. "No one did. Not Susan, not my dad, although I'm not sure he didn't suspect something since he left early that day as well."

"No wonder you got so defensive. I'm sorry I pushed it…. I didn't mean to."

He shook his head and reached out to cup the side of her cheek. "I know. It's not your fault, and I'm so sorry I hurt you."

She turned her head and kissed his hand. "I know."

"I never meant to hurt you." He leaned in and kissed her slowly. He looked into her eyes. "I almost lost you, more than once, and I can't imagine ever living my life without you."

"I…" She shook her head. "Carter…I don't know what to say. There's so much I don't remember."

He pulled back. "I know… I'm pushing. I forget you don't remember everything about who I am."

She shook her head, "I want to…I really do." She winked. "I at least know I'm attracted to you."

He kissed the top of her head. "I know."

"Nate is the only thing I'm sure I remember."

"That son of…"

"Carter, why don't you like him?"

"Because he's after you, plain and simple."

Lily shook her head. "He told me he left his wife."

"That's the whole reason he came here. He came here for you, not for the new book deal."

"Oh, I don't know about that."

"It's true."

She laughed. "He doesn't know what he wants."

"He thinks he does, and he thinks he's a better fit for you than I am."

"Who says I have to choose?"

He shook his head. "You have a point."

She saw the hurt look on his face. "I didn't mean…"

"No, I know what you meant. It's okay."

The door opened. It was Nate.

"Speak of the devil." Carter said under his breath.

"Well, how's my favorite writer doing this morning?" He turned to look at the cowboy at the edge of the bed. "I was hoping I would be able to talk with Lily alone this morning since you're had your chance."

Carter glanced at Lily. "I'll just be out in the waiting room if you need anything."

Lily smiled wistfully and watched as Carter got up and walked out.

"Now that he's gone, we can talk." He sat down next to her. "I know I threw some heavy information at you yesterday. I'm sorry."

Lily shook her head, "It's okay."

"I'm going back to Chicago. You need time to heal, and I need time to… well… I just need time I guess." He took her hand and rubbed the top of it.

"You look pensive."

"A man knows when he's been beat."

"What do you mean?"

"I wanted you for myself."

Lily sighed. "You wanted the dream of me, Nate. Not the real me. I'm a mess."

He brought her hand to his lips and kissed it. "You sell yourself short. You forget, I've known you for a few years now. I know you're a mess."

"Oh, you only know what I let you know. Besides, some catch like you deserves much better than me."

He tilted her chin towards him. "A literary agent and a writer would make the perfect match."

She knew his words held a portion of truth. Yes, Nate was everything she needed. Stability, predictability, and he was sure easy on the eyes with his salt and pepper hair and blue eyes. She also knew he was a man going through a divorce. She didn't want to be the rebound. Besides, she had to figure out what this was with Carter.

She felt something when she was with him that she couldn't quite explain. The two men were opposites ends of the spectrum.

Lily turned her face up as he leaned in and brushed her lips. Although Lily didn't pull back, the kiss felt too platonic. She just didn't feel the same chemistry that she had felt with Carter.

Nate felt it and pulled back, "Well, I guess that answers my question."

Lily shook her head, "I'm sorry. I…"

He shook his head, "I care for you – a lot – but I guess I don't fit the mold for what wins your heart and turns you on."

She closed her eyes. "This is all too much."

"Not for Carter. I saw it, I just thought maybe…" He sighed. "I don't know what I thought. I've got to go." He stood up.

"Nate, don't leave. Not like this. Damnit, I just met you and now you're mad and leaving."

"I'm not mad at you. Not really. My pride is just hurt, that's all," he said as he touched her cheek.

"You believed in me and gave me a chance when no one else would. You mean a lot to me," she told him.

"And you do to me as well," he agreed. "You're a great writer, you know. Don't ever forget that."

"Thank you," she said quietly.

"Look, I've got to get back to Chicago to work on your deal. You just rest up and get better. You've got a lot of edits, writing, and red-carpet appearances to get ready for." He kissed the top of her head. "I'll call when I get back home."

"Alright. Thanks for everything, Nate."

He nodded. "Any time. I'll talk to you soon."

Lily felt a sadness as he walked out of the room. She wanted to feel something more when they kissed but it just didn't happen. At any rate, she at least knew she had a dear friend for life and that was what was important.

As Nate opened the door of the waiting room, Carter stood up.

"Well, you won, Cowboy."

Carter tilted his head. "What do you mean?"

"Let's just say there's not the chemistry I'd hoped for. She loves you."

Carter smirked. "I could say I'm sorry, but I'm not after all the hell you gave me."

Nate chuckled. "I could apologize, but I won't. Just don't break her heart. She's had enough of that. She deserves better."

"You don't have to worry about that. I'll take good care of her."

Nate sighed and stuck out his hand. "You do that."

Carter shook his hand and then asked, "You headed back to Chicago?"

"Yeah, I've got a lot of work to do on our book deal. She's going to be a very busy writer the next year or so. Just remember that, ok?"

Carter nodded.

"Well, I guess I'll be talking to you later."

"Be careful."

Carter stood in the doorway and watched as Nate walked down the hall and then turned the corner. Lily had the chance to choose Nate, but she had chosen him instead. He was one lucky man who had gotten a second chance.

***

Lily saw Mercado stick his head over the stall door at the edge of the barn as they drove by. "Stop the truck." Before the vehicle had come to a complete halt, Lily was already out the door headed for her horse.

"The doctor said take it easy!" Carter called after her as he put the truck in park and scrambled to catch up.

She was already in the stall with her arms wrapped around the yellow gelding's neck when Carter made it to the door.

"As still as he's standing right now, I think he missed you. I had to tie him out every time I picked his stall because he wouldn't stand still."

She chuckled and hugged the horse tighter. "I sure did miss you." She told the horse as she planted a kiss on his cream-colored mane.

"Alright, you've gotten to see him. Let's get you in the house where you can rest."

"Geez, I'm not one of your horses!" she teased as she stepped back and lost her balance slightly.

"Careful. That's why we need to get to the house." He told her as he reached out to steady her.

"I know." She held on to his arm as she closed the stall door. "Thanks for keeping him and letting me stay here."

He lifted her chin so that she had to look at him. "How many times do I have to tell you, Lily Perkins? You're not staying here. This is your home."

She smiled and gave him a kiss. "Thank you."

"You don't have to thank me. You just have to do what I say," he teased.

"You're incorrigible."

"Quit using such big words with me. You know us east Tennessee hillbillies don't understand big words like that!"

She squealed as he scooped her up and took her to the truck.

As they pulled up to the front porch of the log house, Carter told her to sit still. He ran around and lifted her out of the truck.

"What are you doing? I can walk, ya know!"

He flashed a playful grin. "I know."

He carried her up the steps. When he reached the door, he turned the handle and kicked it open with his boot.

"Carter, what are you doing? I'm not an invalid, and it's not like we're married!"

"I know. I just wanted your first night staying here to be special, that's all," he told her as he kissed her forehead.

Who was this crazy cowboy? One minute he was one step away from a Neanderthal and the next he was blowing her away with small gestures such as this.

He promptly carried her to the edge of the bed where he gently sat her down and then pulled the covers back.

She put her feet under as he held the covers. Just as he was standing up, she pulled him to her. "You're not going anywhere, Cowboy."

"Why, whatever do you mean?" he teased.

"This." She kissed him, slowly wrapping her tongue around his, and then pulled him into her.

He tore his mouth away from hers and nipped at her neck as he pinned her arms down. "Nope, you little vixen. I promised the doctor I would make sure you rested, and that's exactly what you're going to do."

"Hmmm…. I kind of like this," she teased.

"Wrong answer," he growled as he planted a kiss on her neck. Her squirming excited him, and he wanted nothing more than to rip her clothes away and feel every curve, but he'd made a promise to himself to wait. She deserved it.

"I'm not overly exerting myself, you know."

He shook his head and stood up. "You need to rest. You've got a big day tomorrow."

She smiled at him. "Alright. Fine."

"Don't you pout on me," He laughed as he planted another kiss on her lips. "Tomorrow will be here before you know it. I'll be right outside if you need anything."

She nodded and settled into the covers. A few minutes later she was sound asleep.

***

"What do you think, Susan?" Lily asked as she pinned up the last stray hair into the vine of daisies in her hair and then checked out her light blue lace dress in the mirror.

She smiled, "Looks perfect to me. I think Carter is going to be blown away. That dress fits you perfectly."

"I sure hope so," she replied as she slipped into a pair of tan scrolled Western boots.

"I'm so glad you two worked it out. I've never seen him so miserable as when you were unconscious. He was out of his head with worry, and guilt. He loves you so much, but I can tell you love him too. That's how it's supposed to be."

"I do love him. I can't help it."

"I guess you found what you were searching for, huh?"

Lily laughed, "Yeah, I guess so. I found my story, but I found so much more."

"By the way, what's the latest on your book?"

"The publisher is releasing Finding Home this fall. I should be done with the script by the first of the year and they'll start filming shortly after that."

"That's great news! I know you're excited."

"Relieved more than anything! I was beginning to question my writing ability. I guess it just took the right place – and the right man- to find my muse."

Susan laughed, "You certainly found the right man." She glanced at her watch. "It's almost time. Are you ready?"

"As ready as I'll ever be."

Lily held on to Susan's arm to keep her steady as they headed to the front door. As Susan opened the door, Lily's heart quickened at the sight of Carter standing tall in his starched Wranglers and long sleeved western shirt, and black felt hat. She'd seen a lot of cowboys in her time, but he was most handsome by far.

"Well, there she is." Carter grinned as he reached for Lily. "This is Preacher Josh. We've known each other since we were kids. He's going to marry us."

Lily nodded. "Nice to meet you."

"So, this is the woman that Carter here has been bragging on. Glad to be of service to you two."

Lily blushed, "Thank you for marrying us. Not a lot of preachers would do that with my um..." She gave a Carter a look of uncertainty.

He came to her rescue. "Background."

"Well, I'm glad Carter finally found someone to settle down with. You both have been through a lot and deserve to be happy."

"I couldn't agree more." Susan added.

"Well, let's get this ceremony started." Josh told them as he led the way to a ring of flowers by the creek that Carter had specially prepared.

Lily took a deep breath as she faced Carter and looked into his dark eyes.

"Carter and Lily, we're here today to celebrate your love for one another as you become one. The relationship you are now entering isn't for a season but for the rest of your lives. To be successful, it will take not only a steadfast love for each another, but trust and commitment, and wanting the best for each other. If you believe this and are truly committed to becoming one, please say, 'I do.'"

Their eyes locked intently, they both said in unison, "I do."

Josh pulled the ring out of his pocket and handed it to Lily. "Lily, place this ring on Carter's finger and repeat after me."

Hands shaking, Lily smiled and pushed the plain gold band on to Carter's finger.

"I, Lily, take joy in committing my life to you. I vow to stand with you as we share this life and cherish the memories we make together."

Never taking her eyes away, Lily repeated the vow to Carter, who winked at her when she finished.

Once again, Josh reached into his pocket and pulled out a simple gold band with a single diamond on the center and handed it to Carter. "Carter, place this ring on Lily's finger and repeat after me."

Carter placed the ring on Lily's finger and then kissed her hand.

"I, Carter, take joy in committing my life to you. I vow to stand with you as we share this life and cherish the memories we make together."

Carter met Lily's gaze full on and repeated the same promise to Lily.

"You have given and received these rings as a symbol of your commitment to love and support one another through all times. We celebrate this union. Now by the power of your love and commitment to each other, and by the power vested in me by the State of Tennessee, I now pronounce you two as husband and wife." Josh grinned. "Carter you can now kiss your bride."

Carter stepped forward and dipped Lily back and grinned. "Hey, wife." Lily giggled nervously but her laughter was replaced by a soft groan as Carter laid a flamboyant kiss on her lips.

"You know, I really thought he'd never find someone." Josh told Susan as they turned and walked towards the house.

"I hoped he would, but I knew it would take one hell of a woman to catch him," Susan replied.

***

Lily gripped Carter's hand and gave him a quick kiss before she stepped in front of the cameras. She smiled and struck a pose on the red carpet against the film festival black drop. The flashes were blinding.

"How does it feel to have a comeback?" One of the reporters yelled over the crowd.

Lily gave Carter a nervous look as she replied, "Good. Very good!"

"When is the baby due?" came a question out of the blue.

Carter reached down and kissed her cheek. "Just go ahead and tell them. They'll find out sooner or later anyhow."

Lily chided him with her look but then answered, "First part of May."

"So, I take it Carter is the cowboy that inspired *Finding Home*?"

Surprising even Lily, Carter stepped up and answered, "Yes, yes I am."

"And it was your town that caught on fire?"

Lily tensed, but her fears quickly faded as Carter calmly answered, "Yes, we did have a fire."

"Thanks everyone, we need to go." Lily told them as she headed for the festival entrance with Carter in tow.

After they were out of earshot of curious journalists, she leaned over and whispered, "You handled that well."

He gave her a roguish grin, "I can do more than just shoe horses, you know."

She reached up and kissed his cheek, "Yeah, I believe I found that out, Cowboy. You're my happiness and my muse and I love you. I finally found what I was searching for."

The End

About F.J. Thomas

A southern gal with a western heart, F.J. Thomas is a multi-genre author and screenwriter who won the Winnie Award for Best Equine Screenplay at the Equus Film Festival. She resides in east Tennessee with the love of her life who is a retired race horse trainer and former professional bull rider T.A. Bouk, and a menagerie of horses, cats, and dogs.

F.J. writes children's picture books under the name Jewel Thomas. Her latest children's book, Beauford The Patriotic Donkey was co-written with T. A. Bouk.

A former OHSA Carded horse show judge, trainer and instructor, F.J. loves competing in anything from huntseat to barrel racing and ranch events every chance she gets. Her articles have appeared in America's Horse, Horse & Ranch Magazine, and Hoofbeats. F.J. writes the motivational and lifestyle blog, Cowgirls With Curves, and the horse-focused writer's blog, Talking In The Barn. Her real life pursuit of the cowgirl lifestyle has provided plenty of first-hand experience and inspiration for writing books a southern twist.

Social Media

IMDB Pro: https://www.imdb.me/F.J.Thomas

Facebook: https://www.facebook.com/fJTHOMASAUTHOR1

Twitter: https://twitter.com/F_J_Thomas @F_J_Thomas

Instagram: https://www.instagram.com/f.j.thomas/

Blogs:
Talking In The Barn -https://fjthomasblog.wordpress.com/
Cowgirls With Curves -http://cowgirlswithcurves.com/

If you enjoyed this story, check out these other Solstice Publishing books by F.J. Thomas:

Lost Betrayal

The future of the ranch hangs in the balance. Sage is just getting her life back together when a tornado touches down and destroys her family ranch in northern Georgia taking her hopes, her dreams and the very horse that the ranch's future hinges on. An ex rodeo cowboy with a past, Garrett has sworn off rodeo and the last thing he needs is entanglement with a woman on a wild horse chase but there's too many unanswered questions, such as how a horse could stay gone so long. Refusing to believe her horse was killed in the storm and refusing to give up on the ranch, Sage begins the journey of rebuilding her life once again and searching for the horse that to her, holds the past and her future. Sordid secrets and malicious betrayal jeopardize her efforts. Is she strong enough to push past the hurt and the lies in order to get back all she holds dear?

https://www.amazon.com/gp/product/B00ISGUJRC/ref=db
s_a_def_rwt_bibl_vppi_i0

Winds on Indian Mound

A typical broke college student, Lacy can't pass up the lure of free board for her horse even if it does mean having to deal with an odd land owner. Undeterred by bizarre old Indian tales, she soon finds out that some deals come at a price, especially when old Indian ghosts come back to life.

https://www.amazon.com/gp/product/B01C66CIJQ/ref=dbs
_a_def_rwt_bibl_vppi_i1

www.ingramcontent.com/pod-product-compliance
Lightning Source LLC
Chambersburg PA
CBHW051139020726
47501CB00005B/1584